# CASTLE REHM

# CASTLE REHM

## THE COMPLETE TRILOGY

Megan Derr

# TABLE OF CONTENTS

# THE SUCCUBUS

Kohar cursed softly in annoyance and pinched the bridge of his nose, careful to avoid touching the nose piece of his rune-scribing monocle. He set his quill aside before he accidentally wrote rat instead of robe, mouth twitching at the image that mistake brought to mind.

Madame Karen would not be amused by the slip.

The horrendous shouting and screaming came again, and he wondered irritably what in the Nether Regions the damnable soldiers were up to now, to cause such a ruckus at this time of morning. The sun wouldn't be up for a couple of hours yet. What sort of trouble could they possibly be into already?

He got up this early because of the peace and quiet, damn it.

The ruckus abruptly subsided, broken up by the sharp, commanding tones of Nerek, Captain of the Guard. Finally.

Picking up his quill, Kohar dipped it into a bottle of deep red, faintly shimmery ink and slowly began to write out runes again—properly this time. He would not be adding water-proofing wards to any rats.

He'd just finished one line when the ruckus started up again—this time much closer. A pounding came at his door as he set the quill down yet again.

"Come in!" he snapped, long familiar with that particular pounding. He rolled his eyes at the phrasing. As if Nerek was interested in giving him that sort of pounding. Nerek was infinitely more likely to knock him upside the head, probably for one flippant remark or another. Kohar was interested in neither option.

The door flew open, and Kohar did not need to turn around to know he was right. Nerek's steps, the jingle-jangle of his sword belt, were as familiar as his knocking. He was likely as rough-looking as ever, in need of a shave, hair with a rampant dislike of combs, leathers scuffed and dirty from whatever was causing all the chaos. He was handsome the way a storm was beautiful—rough, wild, dangerous. They had not been fond of one another when Kohar had first arrived at the castle, but they'd learned to get along, more or less.

"Whatever in the Regions is going on out there," Kohar snapped, still not bothering to turn around, "you had better be putting an end to it. I can't work in all that racket, and one would think even your soldiers could dredge up a bit of consideration given the hour."

"My soldiers never step so much as a toe out of line and you know it. You're a fine one to talk about consideration," Nerek retorted. "Do you think racket would still be going on if there wasn't a good reason for it?"

Kohar rolled his eyes. "Last week there was a ruckus because the chickens got spooked, and let's not forget about the ghost incident."

"I told you not to bring that up anymore."

"You brought it on yourself." Kohar put away the spell he was writing out for Madame Karen, then capped the ink bottles and cleaned his quills before putting them back in their case. He sensed he would be getting very little work done from here on out. A pity.

He had hoped to finish her spells this morning so that he could write a reply to his brother's bizarre letter.

"I do not see how either one of you can be awake at this hour," said another voice. "Even with the current problem."

The voice struck him, sending icy mortification down his spine and hot elation through the rest of him. Damn it all to the Regions, when had Solla arrived, and why had no one told him? Stupid Nerek could have said something! Kohar wasn't remotely dressed for company, still in his bed robe, hair messy, hands and probably his face smudged with ink.

He avoided pitching something heavy at Nerek's head, but only with the greatest of effort. The bastard had done it on purpose, he knew it, and Kohar would make him pay for it.

Kohar finally stood and turned around, forcing back the mortification and annoyance. He loathed that Solla was seeing him at his worst, but he would not compound it by trying to make a fuss or pretend he was something he wasn't. He pushed back a stray curl that had slipped free of the sloppy knot he'd pulled his long hair into while he worked.

Solla was still beautiful. Unlike Nerek, his cousin, who constantly looked rough and unkempt, Solla was always clean and neat. The contrast was all the more notable given that Nerek was Captain of the Guard, and Solla was an aimless mercenary.

Like most natives of Hollar Province, Solla had dark skin, dark hair, and brilliant forest green eyes he had in common with Nerek. Unlike Kohar's long, loose curls and Nerek's shorn, barely-there hair, Solla's hair was shoulder length and held the faintest wave, neatly tied back with a strip of leather. He wore no armor, so he had been there long enough to settle in. From the way he yawned and the somewhat fuzzy look to his eyes, the noise had likely woken him.

Despite that, Solla was fully dressed. Black leggings and a deep red tunic stitched with the moon and cat-head crest of his and Nerek's family. He'd buckled on his sword, and Kohar could see the barest hint of a dagger up his sleeve.

It just made Kohar more painfully aware of his own unkempt state. The same need for perfection that made him so good at magic scribing screamed in fury at being seen in his morning disorder. His fingers twitched with a need to do up the loose fastenings of his bed robe, pull shut the gap that was displaying far too much chest. The only minor consolation he had was that the robe was of deepest midnight blue, matching his eyes exactly. Being from Volane Province, located in roughly the middle of the kingdom, he had white skin, making him and Bedros, the lord of the castle, the odd ones out in the area.

"Why are you bothering me?" he asked again.

Nerek smirked in that way that said he knew exactly what was irking Kohar so much. Well, that was what he got for working with the bastard for so long—they knew entirely too much about each other.

But in the next breath the smirk had faded, Nerek's mouth tightening into a grim line as he fell to business. "Three of my soldiers have been killed by…something…"

"Something?" Kohar asked. He really wished he could get dressed, but that would give away that it bothered him to be seen so, and he refused to make any show of weakness. He quirked a brow instead and used the tone of voice that would make Nerek twitch. "Surely you can muster a better description than 'something', Captain."

Nerek glared. "You want better? Fine. It looks like my soldiers were killed right in the middle of a good session with their hands."

All thoughts of aggravating Nerek and flirting with Solla fled Kohar's mind. "What? Any signs of someone breaking into the castle? Any commonalities between the victims? Any obvious magical traces? There must be something if you're coming to me about it. What do you know so far?"

"No signs of someone breaking into the castle, but that doesn't mean much," Nerek replied, unruffled as ever by Kohar's tendency to rattle off several questions at once. It annoyed everyone else he'd ever met, but it was one of the few things about him Nerek had no complaints for. "Only thing they had in common was that they work for me. One works the curtain, the second is on bodyguard rotation, and the last is a field scout. Can't be certain it's magical in nature, but there was no sign of anything else, not even another person, despite the awkward way they died."

Kohar frowned, absently doing up the last few fastenings on his robe and smoothing it out. Moving to his wardrobe, he dug out his leather boots and sat to tug them on. Standing, he took off his monocle and forced his hair into submission, swearing softly when he could not locate the comb that held it all together. He stopped when he saw a hand holding it out and smiled at Solla. "Thank you."

Solla nodded, smiling briefly, then stepped back.

Retrieving his monocle, he settled it in place, twitching his nose to get it just right, then motioned for Nerek to lead the way.

The castle halls were cold; it would be some hours yet before the sun was high enough to warm them. He should have grabbed his cloak, but did not waste time on fetching it. Normally at such an hour, everything would be dead silent. On the rare occasion he left his room at this time, Kohar seldom encountered any but one of the watchmen or Nerek. Where Kohar had always enjoyed being awake in the deadest hours of the morning, Nerek had no choice in the matter and was absolutely never happy about it.

Today, however, the castle was already alive—and teeming with fear. Servants stood muttering and whispering about what the problem might be, what was becoming of those damned soldiers, and it was only a matter of time before His Grace woke.

He followed Nerek and Solla across the courtyard to the barracks, where the soldiers stood milling fretfully. Their eyes were filled with terror—and anger. They seemed comforted, though, when they saw him, their whispers subsiding as he stepped past them into the room.

Kohar's eyes immediately fell on the only bed in the room still occupied. The soldier was dead, but his eyes were wide open, as was his mouth, the whole of his face strangely contorted in a grimace of pleasure and pain.

He frowned at the unfortunate state in which the man seemed to have died—his tunic discarded, leggings open, cock lying spent with his hands still wrapped around it, drying semen on his stomach.

"There's two more," Nerek said into the silence. "So far, is my fear."

"Let's hope not," Kohar murmured, focused now on finding any traces of magic that he could.

His monocle was intended primarily for rune scribing. Basic spells were simple enough they could be spoken, even certain moderately complex spells were so familiar that speaking them was safe enough. But everything else had to be written, and writing magic was a skill that took a bare minimum of twenty years of training—ten basic, ten specialized. Kohar had started at nine, finished at thirty. Even now at thirty-five, it remained a difficult, dangerous task.

To the naked eye, runes were no more complicated than ordinary penmanship. Beneath the monocle, however, the special inks came to life, where the slightest variation in a stroke could mean the difference between glorious success and horrific failure. It showed him where to make a mark lighter or darker, where to curve, where to keep it straight, where to wing it sharply, and that didn't even get into the different colors of ink required. There were thousands of nuances, resulting in a craft so challenging that precious few were able to obtain their master marks. The monocle was one of his dearest possessions and had not come cheaply.

And the things that made it crucial for writing magic also made it useful at simply seeing magic, at least some of it—like now, in lingering traces of a rune marked on the unfortunate soldier's neck, right where fingers might caress, rest before drawing someone in for a kiss, or squeeze in a friendly gesture. It was tiny, small enough to fit on a fingertip. Frowning, Kohar moved in close enough to gently touch the mark with one finger.

His finger came away greasy, and he thoughtfully rubbed his thumb and forefinger together, then brought them to his nose to sniff. "Rune wax," he said. Most of the spells he wrote were for other mages; he simply left off the last couple of runes, gave them the incomplete spell, and they finished it when the spell was needed. That was what he did for Madame Karen, the village healer, whose eyesight kept her from being able to be a master scriber. She could always add the last rune or two just fine, but not the full spell.

But on those occasions where it wasn't a mage who needed the spell, they were written in full, transferred into special rune wax, and then activated, essentially putting the spell in stasis. From there, the spell could be transferred to a desired location by anyone, not just a mage. But rune wax was prohibitively expensive, and transferring live spells incredibly dangerous. There were few good reasons to do it when it was safer and cheaper to simply hire a mage to do the spell at the required location but plenty of bad reasons.

"Wonderful," Nerek said. "So whoever the scum is, you can't sniff out their magic."

"Unfortunately not. Show me the other two."

Nerek did so. The second was a woman who'd died with one hand shoved up her shirt and the other into her pants, and the third a man who'd died with one hand on his cock, and two fingers of the other buried in his ass.

"No one deserves to die this way," Nerek said. "It's humiliating, violating. I don't know what sick bastard is responsible, but I'm going to cut out their delicate bits and shove them down their throat."

"I do not usually approve of your crude methods, but in this case I'd be willing to make an exception. In fact, I think you're being too kind."

Worry and even a touch of fear slipped over Nerek's face for a moment. "What in the Regions are we dealing with?"

"I would have to consult my books to be certain, but to judge from the state of them and the faded runes on their skin, I think we have a concubus feeding on your men."

"What's a concubus?" Solla asked, speaking for the first time.

Kohar didn't roll his eyes, but it was a near thing. "You might be more familiar with the term 'succubus.'"

Solla laughed, a touch of derision in it. "You think we're dealing with a demon."

It stung. A lot. Solla had been dropping by to visit Nerek for years, since long before Kohar had arrived. He visited infrequently, only a handful of times a year, and only a day or three at a time, but often enough he should not be so quick to disbelieve what Kohar had to say.

"Yes, I do," Kohar said icily.

Solla looked at him with disappointment, then looked to Nerek. "You can't believe him."

"Of course I do."

The disappointment grew. "You yell at him over everything. You ignore him when he claims rats are getting at his books again, but you believe him about something as impossible as a demon."

"Yes, I do," Nerek said again, voice dropping several degrees.

Kohar ignored the way that unflappable confidence warmed him better than any tea, because honestly, what did he care whether or not Nerek believed him? He was right, that was all that mattered. "It's high magic, not impossible magic, and it's the only thing that fits."

"Why?" Nerek interrupted, giving his cousin a warning look. "That is what I want to know."

"You have to ask?" Kohar said dryly. "After the failed betrothal?"

Nerek sighed, running a hand over his shorn hair and then down his face. "I had hoped that after three months of peace and quiet, we didn't have to worry about revenge from that quarter anymore."

Kohar murmured a soft agreement. He and Nerek were in the employ of the Duke of Rehm, helping to guard the largely ignored and forgotten northeast corner of the kingdom. Three months ago, the

Countess of Greesom had arrived to finalize a betrothal with His Grace.

It had come as a shock to all of them when His Grace had abruptly called the whole thing off and thrown her out. Her Ladyship had taken the news neither gracefully nor quietly.

"I cannot see who else would do this," Kohar continued. "Though it lacks refinement. I would have thought Her Ladyship would be less crude. Now I'm really curious as to why he threw her out."

Nerek shrugged. "As mad as she was, I doubt being refined was high on her list of concerns. I suppose we had better confirm it before we go raze her damned palace."

"You? Think?" Kohar asked. "I'm impressed you can manage it this ear—"

A sudden scream cut him off, and at the far end of the long barracks, a wave of men surged toward them, bellowing for Nerek, motioning, bolting away as quickly as they could.

Nerek shut everyone up with a bellow.

"Wake up anyone who might still be asleep," Kohar ordered as they took in the latest victim. "Succubi can only feed on the sleeping. Make certain everyone bathes—thoroughly. Tell them all to be on guard against anyone—anyone—trying to touch their bare skin."

Noise exploded around him as the men took in Kohar's words, more than a few of the soldiers making the motions to ward against demons, and hastily muttered prayers mingled with the chatter.

Leaving Kohar's side, Nerek set to work calming the men down, issuing orders and sending some of them out to spread those orders throughout the castle. In mere minutes, the barracks were empty, and soon the sounds of soldiers at drill and chores filled the castle.

Rubbing his forehead, longing for a cup of tea, Kohar forced himself to focus.

The Countess was not the immediate problem, though she was the likeliest source of the problem. No, the immediate problem was finding and expelling the damned demon.

"How is one demon killing this many people?" Nerek asked as he returned.

"Precisely," Solla said. "How could it possibly be a demon? What's it doing, jumping from dream to dream?"

"Yes, exactly," Kohar said. "It's called a chain spell. My brother studies them, amongst other things. A demon is summoned and bound into a series of runes that have been chained together. So it's bound to the first one, and when that rune is used up or destroyed, it jumps to the next one, and so on until it comes to the end of the spell, or all the runes are otherwise destroyed." He turned to Nerek. "We have a rat. It takes a mage at least as good as I to summon a succubus, and I would know if another of my caliber was around. Someone here is depositing the spells on behalf of that mage."

"I was afraid of that," Nerek said with a sigh, rubbing one hand along the side of his chin, looking angry and tired but still somehow scruffily handsome.

Kohar wondered absently, for likely the millionth time, why the man rarely bothered to shave. One would think Nerek would enjoy something that involved a sharp knife, given how many of them he carried about his person.

"The men are allowed leave on a regular rotation; I'll check the logs and see who was in the last batch. We're likeliest to find our rat amongst them." He looked at his cousin. "Unless Solla is up to something, but he's still too asleep to be committing crimes."

For reply, Solla yawned. "I am up to murdering a large breakfast, but that's about it."

Kohar nodded. "By all means, seek out food; this is not your problem."

Smiling faintly, Solla nodded, gripped Nerek's shoulder, then left the barracks in search of food.

"Lazy bastard," Nerek muttered.

Ignoring the complaint because he knew damn good and well Nerek was just jealous Solla would get to enjoy food and rest, Kohar swatted Nerek's arm and made him focus. "Lists, you lummox, get the lists. Who was on leave? Who left? Who stayed? Who traded out?"

"It's against the rules to trade duty assignments without permission from me," Nerek said and sighed. "Which means at least ten of the bastards did it. Come on, we'll look'em all over." Bellowing a last few orders at the senior officers overseeing the removal of the bodies, he led the way to his office.

Inside, wonderful smells wafted over him. Kohar's stomach growled as he took in the food set out—simple bread and cheese and hot cider, but it looked a feast to him. Enough for two, so the cooks had known he'd be here. "See, you get food after all. No reason to be jealous of Solla."

Nerek's scowl just darkened as he strode across the room and started shuffling through papers on the table near his desk.

Kohar strode to the desk and stole Nerek's seat, pulling the platters close and helping himself. Picking up a mug of cider, he watched Nerek work. For all the man perpetually looked like a grizzled soldier who hadn't seen civilization in years, his office was always neater than a monk's cell and smelled of sweet incense.

"Here we are," he said after a few minutes, then

yanked the hunk of bread out of Kohar's hand. He motioned to the papers as he picked up the second mug. "All good men. I cannot picture them as being responsible for something like this." He shook his head.

"It's always the one you least expect," Kohar murmured.

Nerek grunted. "True enough. Look at what a family of merchants and tavern owners produced." He smirked at Kohar.

Ignoring him, Kohar flipped through the lists. He knew most of the names. It was hard not to know them, being the only mage-in-residence and working closely with the soldiers. Sadness and anger washed through him. "Why would they do it?"

"The Countess is a damned pretty woman."

A flicker of annoyance passed through Kohar, though he couldn't say why. The Countess was pretty—beautiful, in fact. No one could understand why His Grace had turned her down at the last moment, and he had never seen fit to explain—not even to Kohar and Nerek.

"Maybe I should be examining you," he said sourly. "Did you fall beneath the wiles of the Countess, Captain?"

"I wouldn't kill my own men," Nerek said, voice cold.

Kohar winced. "I know. Sorry, it was an ill-thought jest."

Nerek glanced down at the lists and sighed. "To be fair, one of my men is responsible, so somebody couldn't resist the woman's tits."

"Were her tits that remarkable?" Kohar hadn't actually noticed. Women had never done anything for him. But he was fairly certain they did plenty for Nerek and His Grace.

"They were perfect. His Grace was an absolute

fool to throw that away." He threw the papers down. "Speaking of which, you'd better go speak with him."

"About her tits?" Kohar muttered, annoyed all over again, though Regions if he knew why. What did he care if Nerek thought some angry woman's tits were perfect? At Nerek's glare, he heaved to his feet. "I'm going, I'm going." He ate the last of the bread and drained his cider. "Make certain you leave no detail out when questioning the men. If they are not guilty, perhaps they might have unwittingly spied some clue. Surely someone saw something last night or this morning that would help us."

"I know how to do my job. Stop fussing." Nerek reclaimed his seat and sent Kohar an admonishing look before he called for the aide waiting patiently in the hall.

Brushing crumbs from his robe, smoothing back a loose strand of hair, Kohar departed and made his way back to the main keep. Servants ran to and fro now, busily tending to the morning chores. The faintest threads of gray were beginning to lighten the sky, though it would not be true light for a little while yet, especially given the perpetual clouds this time of year. He stopped a passing maid who was carrying a heavy tray of food. "Is His Grace awake?"

"Yes, Master Kohar. I was just taking him breakfast."

"I'll take it. I need to speak with him, and it'll save you a trip up those stairs, eh?"

She beamed and handed it over. "Thank you, Master Kohar."

"You and the others can all leave off the 'Master' you know. I think we've been stuck together in this castle long enough."

She giggled, waggled her fingers in goodbye, and dashed off to see to the rest of her morning chores.

Kohar smiled briefly and then headed down the hall then up the enormous northern staircase, the tray balanced in one hand, a skill acquired from the years he'd spent working in his aunt's tavern.

Halfway down the hall that led to His Grace's private solar, however, the door to one of the spare bedrooms opened and Solla stepped out into the hall. Kohar smiled. "Did you manage to find breakfast, then?'"

"Of course," Solla said with a smile. His smiles were always so pretty. Unlike Nerek, who might have pretty smiles, but nobody would know because all the man did was scowl. "Did you have any luck so far with finding your culprit?"

"Not yet, but we've barely begun. Nerek is going through his men now to try and roust the rat," Kohar replied. "I am off to report to His Grace. I'm afraid you've come at a particularly bad time, between the murders, the demon committing them, and of course all this snow. How did you even reach us through all of it?"

Solla smiled again, but this time it was slow and burning, a bit of an unmistakable gleam in his eye. "I had the motivation." He stepped in closer, reaching out to curl his fingers around Kohar's wrist—and getting briefly distracted as he looked down and saw that Kohar's sleeve came all the way up to his knuckles, even looping over his thumb and one finger. Then he seemed to shake himself, and let go after a gentle, fleeting caress to the inside of Kohar's wrist. "Sorry, it just seems so clever. You're much warmer than I am in this drafty castle." That slow, hot smile again. "Anyway, I wanted to apologize for doubting you earlier. It just seems so unbelievable that there could be a real, actual demon running around. Do you think I could be in danger?"

"Best to assume so," Kohar replied, pleasure running through him at the apology. "Like we ordered all the soldiers and staff: scrub yourself thoroughly and be careful of being touched on bare skin by anyone."

Solla's smile widened into a mischievous grin. "I'll be sure to wash everything thoroughly."

"Um. Yes. Good idea." A tingle ran along Kohar's spine. If only he had time for Solla and his sudden, delightful interest. What had changed? Seeing Kohar in his bedrobe? Doubtful. "If you will excuse me for now, I do not want to keep His Grace waiting."

"By all means," Solla said, sketching a brief bow. "I will see you later, Kohar."

Indeed he would. Kohar forced himself to calm down as he continued on down the hall. After all this time, Solla was finally noticing him. Regions, he'd given up doing anything but admiring since Nerek had gleefully informed him that Solla had only ever expressed interest in women.

Maybe stupid Nerek didn't know his cousin as well as he thought.

Smiling faintly, helplessly thinking of all the fun they would have once this succubus problem was resolved, Kohar knocked lightly on His Grace's door and pushed it open as a bid to enter was called.

Bedros, the Duke of Rehm, was one hundred percent noble Volarian. Pale white skin, dark blue-gray eyes, ink-black hair still in its messy sleeping braid. Tall, broad in the chest and shoulders, and currently he wore only an old pair of leggings and a faded violet tunic. He'd tugged on light leather house boots, but that was all. He was beautiful—breathtaking—even if he unfortunately shared Nerek's tendency towards always looking rough and unkempt. Maybe they'd just conceded defeat to the inhospitable environment and were trying to mimic it, instead of doing constant battle to look civilized like Kohar.

Sitting at his table, Bedros motioned him forward and said, "I hear there is a succubus on my premises."

"I see the gossip mills are still functioning flawlessly," Kohar said dryly, setting the breakfast tray on the table near the fireplace. "Yes, Your Grace. Nerek and I are currently attempting to locate the culprit." He quickly explained what they knew; sadly, it took only a moment.

Grunting, Bedros began to eat, doing so quickly and neatly. "Tell me everything you know about succubi, Kohar."

Kohar frowned, brows drawing sharply down. "Not much, I'm afraid. Demons are specialized magic, and I pursued much more mundane paths."

"Mundane, yes, to write out delicate spellwork all day with a special license that took two decades of work to get," Bedros said, casting him an amused look over the rim of his cup.

"Well I certainly can't do anything as exciting as summoning murderous demons to slaughter unsuspecting soldiers who just wanted to masturbate in peace," Kohar replied, making Bedros choke on his cider. "Anyway, this is what I do know: They are part of a fornication class of demons, class one or two, I don't remember which. They feed on lust. They're non-corporeal demons, which means they have no physical form in the mortal world. They can interact with humans only via dreams, where they become what the victim most lusts after and drain their life energy away via fornication."

Bedros's brows furrowed. "I see. So are all my people in danger? Or solely those that, what, have a sexual interest in women? Do we know?"

"It doesn't really matter. Succubus is simply the

term most people know, since men do love their tales of being helplessly seduced by a beautiful woman who wants to kill them."

"I wish I could say you were wrong," Bedros said, rolling his eyes. "So what's the right term?"

"It depends. Concubus is the one most often used by mages. Before we understood it enough to know it was genderfluid in nature, it was mistakenly believed to be two different beings–the succubus that preys on those who prefer women, and the incubus that preys on those who prefer men. And it could of course be either for those whose tastes are not so limited."

"Interesting," Bedros said. "You say it's only a class one or two? What could possibly rank above a demon that kills men and women with lust?"

"Trust me when I say you never want to find out."

"I believe you." Bedros drummed his fingers on the table. "Have I pissed off anyone besides the Countess in recent history?"

"If you did, I haven't heard of it," Kohar replied. "Certainly no one capable of this level of magic or with sufficient funds to hire someone who has it. This kind of magic would cost enough money even you would wince."

"I see," Bedros said. "I could be wrong, gods know I was wrong about plenty where Lady Greesom was concerned, but I never heard anything about her knowing magic, never mind being capable of summoning demons."

Kohar frowned. That had not occurred to him. They had leapt immediately to the Countess as the culprit but had not stopped to consider if she knew magic. "She very likely has at least a few mages-in-residence."

Bedros snorted. "Kohar, if I told you to

summon a demon that would kill several people, all for the sake of petty revenge over a broken betrothal, what would you do?"

"Tell you to take yourself to the Regions," Kohar replied. "Your revenge isn't worth my life and livelihood." Even leaving aside the matter of his life, his skills and reputation were far too precious to throw away on someone else's wounded pride. "So if it is the Countess, then she is hiring a disreputable mage to do the summoning, who in turn had the sense, regrettably, to send someone else to do the actual casting. That explains a bit, but nothing terribly useful."

"This doesn't really seem her style, and I don't see why she'd get revenge via setting a succubus on my soldiers. That seems personal, and we were never that involved."

Kohar looked at him. "Her style. May I ask, Your Grace, why you severed the betrothal?" More dryly he added, "Nerek thinks you were a perfect fool to throw away such perfect tits."

"She did have lovely breasts—lovely everything, really, except for her willingness to do anything for power." Bedros sighed. "My reason is not that interesting, in the end, which is why I never bothered to say anything before. There's not really much to say. I used to be good friends with His Majesty before he abruptly found himself on the throne when the rest of his family was felled by that plague that went around several years ago. Power has not, shall we say, been good for him?"

"No, it has not," Kohar replied, mouth flattening. Their current king was a power-hungry cretin who would probably have the country going to full out war before the year was out, despite all the protestations of his council and people.

"There was a man neither of us liked much, who

is frankly a bastard himself. His Majesty tried to make him take the fall for the crimes of one of his toadies. The penalty would have been execution. I saved him and forced the toady to answer for his own crimes. It is only because we are old friends that I was essentially exiled here instead of being executed myself—one way or another. Her Ladyship was a chance to redeem myself. Marry her, do what I was told, and I'd be welcomed back to the royal palace and friends with the king once more. I tried to go through with it but ultimately could not."

"I never realized." Kohar stared at him with newfound respect, though he'd already thought highly of a man who treated his servants with respect and always listened to what Kohar and Nerek said when advising him, instead of assuming his station meant he knew more than either of them. "I'm sorry."

Bedros waved the words aside. "The point is that you can see why I don't think the Countess is behind this. She was another tool, one more ambitious and malleable than I, but a tool all the same. She's likely already moved on to a more amenable pawn. Why waste gold and risk imprisonment over a marriage she doesn't actually care about?"

"Then who else?" Kohar asked. "Surely no one across the border would attempt this. As you say, it is a costly venture." He could feel the beginnings of a headache.

Bedros shrugged. "I don't know. Until we figure it out, we will focus our energies on fighting the demon." He looked up, dark brown eyes serious. "We will support you as best we can, of course, but it's magic we fight, so it's all on you." He smiled ruefully. "I suppose we had best see about finally hiring on some help for you."

"I will do my best, Your Grace. As to help, I get

by just fine. It's not like there's usually much to do around here. I'll work as quickly as I can, but demons are well outside my purview, so it will take some research."

He received a dismissive wave. "Do whatever is necessary. But be certain to get dressed first, Kohar. I'm amazed you haven't frozen to death running around in nothing but that robe of yours. Never mind you must be distracting Nerek like crazy."

Kohar rolled his eyes. "I think Nerek is a touch too busy to be mad about my lack of proper clothing. He doesn't tend to care what I wear on a good day."

Bedros quirked a brow at him but said nothing, merely returned to his breakfast and the pile of reports and missives regarding other matters in the keep and territory.

Dismissed, Kohar returned quickly to his own room. Clearly heeding the edict about washing, someone had left him a pitcher of hot water and cleaning rags. Stripping out of his robe, he quickly washed down, then pulled on fresh underclothes before unclipping his hair.

Picking up his comb, he began the process of untangling and combing his long, loose curls. Damn his father anyway; Kohar had wished all his life to possess his mother's perfectly straight hair. Thinking of his parents made him think of his younger brother, Taniel, who was all the family he had left now. His eldest sister, a traveler, had died climbing a mountain. Only a few years after that, the plague had taken their parents, remaining siblings, and all the relatives they cared about. A merchant company a century old and a tavern nearly as old, gone like that. His brother was a monk now, studying the sort of high level, esoteric magic Kohar had never cared about. A pity he was too far away; likely he'd know far more about demons than

Kohar.

That reminded him he'd never gotten a chance to reply to Taniel's…

Taniel's letter. It couldn't be. Striding across the room, Kohar snatched it up and reread it again.

*Dear Kohi,*

*I hope this letter reaches you in time. I am afraid that much has happened here at the monastery, but the short explanation is that I have made someone incredibly angry, and unfortunately he was able to escape custody. He has vowed revenge, and regrettably I told him all about you long before I realized his true nature.*

*Please be careful. I do not know what form his revenge will take, but I'm certain it will focus on you. I will be there as soon as I can, but I worry the weather will impede me. I beg of you, take this warning seriously and have utmost care. I do not want to lose you too.*

*Love,*
*Tani*

"Shit! Shit, shit, shit!" Tossing aside the letter, Kohar hastened to finish dressing. He bound his hair in a knot at the back of his head, securing it with a sharply pointed comb carved from jade. Then he went to the wardrobe and quickly pulled on leggings and a long-sleeved white shirt. Over this he drew a floor-length tunic split up the center in both front and back to about mid-thigh. It was dark blue, the edges meticulously embroidered with dark gray thread in a diamond pattern. A belt of supple black leather wrapped twice around his waist, and to this he attached his keys and various other things he would need throughout the course of the day.

He sat down to draw on his knee-high boots, then retrieved his monocle and tucked it into a special pocket of his tunic. Then he snatched the letter up and raced off.

"Where's Nerek?" he asked the first soldier he saw.

"The-uh-the armory," the soldier replied.

Kohar thanked him even as he started running again, bolting down the hall and shoving open the door that led to a set of stairs that spilled into the eastern ward. Swearing loudly at the biting cold, he took the stairs as quickly as he dared—and slipped, going down painfully and sliding the rest of the way, landing in a heap of pain and mortification at the bottom.

"You dumbass!" came Nerek's familiar voice, and before Kohar could reply, he was being pulled to his feet, dusted off, and roughly checked over. "Are you all right?"

"Fine, I'm fine," Kohar said, cheeks burning with shame, his back and right arm burning with agony. "Never mind me, I know who is behind this—well, not really, but sort of." Before Nerek could voice the scathing opinion painted on his face, he shoved the crumpled, snow-covered letter he still held into Nerek's chest. "My brother pissed someone off, someone he's scared of. I think that might be the source of our trouble."

"Kohi?" Nerek said as he started reading, giving him a faintly amused look before all traces of it vanished as he continued reading. Then he grabbed Kohar's arm and dragged him across the ward, his spiked boots doing a much better job of handling the snow and ice than Kohar's ordinary ones.

Once they were in the armory, and he'd shoved Kohar down onto a stool close to the fire, he pulled up a stool of his own and said, "You really think your brother is the reason my people are dying? What do my soldiers have to do with a bunch of monks?"

"Nothing, and that is probably the point. Whoever this is, whatever is going on, they are hurting us—all of us—to get back at my brother. If I had to guess, I'd say I'm meant to watch the suffering before suffering myself. Something like that. It's how this sort of nonsense usually goes."

Nerek quirked a brow. "How often do you and your brother piss people off?"

"Not us," Kohar said. "My parents do—did, I mean, before the plague took them and the business. They were unusually ethical for merchants, and that somehow managed to make a lot of people angry, especially employees they caught doing untoward things. My siblings and I were jumped by footpads more than once while going about town."

The humor on Nerek's face vanished. "I'm sorry. You never mentioned your family was dead. Just spoke about them being merchants and tavern owners."

Kohar shrugged. "I don't like to talk about it. We were a family of six—nineteen if you include the relatives we actually talked to and cared about. Now there's just two of us."

There was one of those awful, heavy silences, then Nerek reached out and cupped his cheek, the leather of his gloves warm and surprisingly soft. His green eyes were soft, full of more understanding and sympathy than Kohar could bear. "I'm sorry."

"It was years ago," Kohar said, looking away. "But thank you. The point is, my brother seems to have inherited their knack for pissing people off."

"Oh, I think it's more than him," Nerek muttered, but at Kohar's glare, only said, "I don't suppose there's any way to get more information?"

Kohar shook his head. "No, unfortunately, not

until he's able to reach us, and that will be far too late. Our original plan is still our best chance: I need to go to the library and do some research on how to hunt out a demon, while you try to roust out the rat."

Nerek ran a hand down his face. "Fine. I wish we had more to work with, but I suppose any start is better than none. Have you told Bedros yet?"

"No, I thought you needed to know first."

"I'll tell him. You get to work on your research. And take something for all the bruises you just gave yourself."

"Never fear, lord and master," Kohar replied, "I won't impede progress with my hobbling around the castle in abject misery."

"That's not—" Nerek heaved a sighed. "Never mind." He stood and stormed off, calling out to a couple of soldiers to attend him.

"What was that all about?" Kohar asked no one in particular. He stood more slowly, wincing at the bruises he could already feel forming, his back and right arm throbbing, stiff with pain. But he'd just have to endure, because healing tonics made him sleepy. Not to mention there weren't many left, and he needed the weather to clear up a bit before he could make more, since the kitchen staff hated when he commandeered any of their space to work, and he needed more than his work room for a project as large as tonics.

He was nearly to the door when a soldier shyly approached, holding out a pair of boots that had been shined to within a thread of their life. Kohar had never understood how Nerek could look so scruffy all the time but saw to it everyone under his command never looked less than pristine. "Can I help you?"

"Captain told me to give you these, and said you're to wear them, else he'll hunt you down and make you."

"Make me, huh?" Kohar didn't know why that made him feel hot and squirmy, and he didn't have the time to figure it out, even if he wanted to. He knew an earnest threat when he heard it though. "I see. Thank you, Private." He sat on one of the benches by the door and with the private's help, removed his own boots and got the new ones on and laced up. They were soldier's boots, heavy and fur-lined, with the reinforced toe and the special ice-spikes already strapped into place. "He does know I'm not one of his soldiers, right?"

The woman laughed. "Captain hands out orders to everyone. I'm pretty sure he'd order his own mother around if she was here."

That, Kohar actually knew to not be true. Unlike Kohar's parents, who had loved and supported him his whole life—until they'd lost theirs, anyway—Nerek's father was a nonexistent figure in his life and his lifelong soldier mother saw his dull posting and lack of ambition as a monumental failure and personal affront. Nerek had never actually said, but Kohar's impression was that they hadn't spoken in years.

Shunting aside errant thoughts of Nerek's worthless, unappreciative mother, Kohar rose and tested out the boots. "Thank you. Hopefully now I'll have better luck going up the stairs than I did coming down them."

Smiling in understanding, the private replied, "If it makes you feel any better, he went tail over teakettle this morning helping the staff haul in firewood."

"That makes me feel infinitely better, thank you. You're my favorite person in the whole world."

She giggled, and with a parting evil grin, Kohar headed back out into the wretched cold. Thankfully, this time he traversed the stairs successfully, though not a stitch of him was left uncovered by the time he got inside again. Shaking off the snow, blowing on his poor fingers to get the feeling back in them—he really needed to find his missing gloves—he headed for the library.

Unfortunately, the library had slim offerings. Many of the books in it were those Kohar had brought with him when he'd been assigned to Rehm Castle. He hadn't been overjoyed with the posting. Quite the opposite. He'd been hoping to go to one of the great libraries, or at least a place that offered more than a freezing castle, a village that spent half the year drinking beer and the other half drinking cider, with the odd mead thrown in for fun, and a relationship with the village on the other side of the border that would not amuse the throne. It was where they got the cider, along with apples, traded for beer and honey. The only thing they all loved more than drinking was tumbling one another in the nearest haystack or barn, and gossiping about the whole mess when they all finally woke up.

Unfortunately, for all he had a damned fine collection—many of the volumes gifts from his parents and sister—they were focused on history, runes, and rune scribing. He'd known what he wanted to do practically from the start, and so had never bothered with volumes that focused on high level magic and the sort of esoteric stuff his brother loved.

What in the world had Taniel done that someone would go to this much trouble for revenge? For starters, the monastery where Taniel lived was at least two months away in good weather. But starting in late fall, successfully making it from one to the other was best described as a miracle. To also summon a demon, bind it to a chain spell, set it in rune wax, and pay someone to do the hard part?

That wasn't just alarming sums of money, it was significant amounts of time, and if the culprit was caught alive, they were guaranteed to have their head separated from their body by way of a large axe.

The first book he pulled down was a general bestiary of magical creatures. Simply understanding the way they were indexed took a year or two of intense study, never mind the cross referencing and copious footnotes and bibliographies. Flipping deftly through the pages, he quickly came to what he sought.

Reading over the information provided told him nothing he did not already know, but it did tell him where to look for what he needed. Luckily, he had one of the five books listed that would address the matter. Returning the bestiary to its place, he pulled down the book it had referenced.

There, that was everything he needed to know: how the demon was summoned, how it could be located, and how to banish it. That was the good news.

The bad news was that he lacked all the components he needed to find and expel the damned thing. He might be able to make the inks for the finding, but the three he needed for the expelling required items he did not keep around because they were too dangerous, too expensive, or both. This was what he got for being a boring mage living in a valley full of drunks.

The threatened headache throbbed at his temples, making him nauseous, making the world too sharp, too bright. Kohar gritted his teeth and ignored it as best he could. Headaches and bruised backsides would have to wait their turn; he had too much else to deal with right now.

He waited for the ink to dry on his notes, leaning back in his seat and staring up at the ceiling. This entire mess was ruining his schedule. It would take him days to catch up on the work he'd hoped to accomplish. Madame Karen was going to kill him—

slowly—for not having her spells finished on time. She was an infrequent client, but one who paid well. And she did not approve of anything being late. Even her children had all known full well to be born on time.

She would just have to suffer, though. People were dying. Everything else could wait.

Standing, he picked up his notes and rolled the scrap of paper up, securing it with a piece of string and tucking it beneath his tunic. Nerek was likely—

He oofed as he crashed into something. Rubbing his nose, which throbbed painfully with the impact, Kohar glared up at whomever he'd run into—and his irritation promptly vanished. "My apologies, I should have looked where I was going."

"Not at all," Solla replied. "The fault is entirely my own." He reached out to gently touch Kohar's face, brushing a thumb over his cheekbone, lingering a moment. "I accidentally snuck up on you. I wanted to see how your hunt for information was going."

"Good, not great," Kohar replied, resisting an urge to rub his sore nose again. He hoped it wasn't bright red or anything. That was all he needed, to look like a great buffoon now that he was finally getting the sort of attention from Solla he'd always hoped for. "I need to speak with Nerek—"

"Nerek this, Nerek that," Solla said. "You two spend more time talking about each other than anything else, even dead bodies."

"What is that supposed to mean?"

Solla touched his cheek again, fingers rough and cool. "It means, I'd rather talk about—"

"Yourself, no doubt," Nerek cut in, voice at least as frigid as the weather. "Am I the only one getting any work done around here?"

"Shut up before I smack you upside the head with one of my books," Kohar replied, nudging Solla out of the way and pulling out the scrap of paper he'd just tucked into his tunic. "Here, this is what I found, as I was just coming to tell you."

Nerek looked over the list. "Is this supposed to mean something to me, other than a very expensive shopping list?"

"Ugh, soldiers." Kohar snatched the list back and pointed. "It says right here! Locating! Expelling! I need these components for the inks I need to write these spells. I think I can manage the locating, but I definitely don't know how to come by the missing components for the expelling, so we'll have to figure out a way to trap the demon somewhere until I can get them. I'm still working on that part. But first I have to go into the village to get the missing components for the locating spell."

"That's good timing, then, because I might have a lead on a culprit for us," Nerek said. His green eyes were hard as stone as he stared first at Solla and then Kohar. "It appears one of my soldiers is missing; apparently she often sneaks away to visit her sweetheart in the village. She's been doing it for months."

No wonder Nerek was in such a foul mood. Nothing angered him like foolish disobedience. "I'm guessing she's still in the village?"

"Yes. I was going to see if you wanted to come along, simply because you might see something I wouldn't. Now we can get your components as well."

Kohar nodded. "Let me get my cloak."

"Meet me in the courtyard." Glaring at them both one last time, Nerek turned sharply on his heel and stalked off.

"I don't know how you put up with that all the time," Solla said.

"Put up with what? Nerek? Being angry

because people are dead?"

"He's like that all the time, let's be honest here."

Kohar frowned at him, the expectant look on his face, an unpleasant squirming in his gut. Because Nerek might be cranky and scruffy and bossy, but he was also kind, funny, and worked twice as hard as anyone else. He could be difficult to deal with at times, yes, but so could Kohar. So could Bedros. So could anyone who worked in a castle that spent more time covered in snow and ice than not. "I need to go, excuse me please."

He hastened out of the library, tucking his notes away again, ignoring when Solla called after him. Hurrying to his room, he fetched his heavy, fur-trimmed wool cloak

When he reached the courtyard a few minutes later, Nerek was still all but vibrating with anger.

"You know, the last thing we need right now is you losing your temper," Kohar said as he mounted his horse, a white mare that had been his welcome gift from Bedros.

Nerek jerkily shrugged his shoulders. "You are flirting and playing with my cousin while my people are dying. I'm allowed to be pissed off about it."

"Now see here—" Kohar said, but Nerek was already riding off, leaving him to fume as he tried to catch up.

It took several minutes, as Kohar's mare was meant for leisurely rides into the village on nice days, and Nerek rode a courser that shared a lot of attitude problems with its master.

In the distance, smoke curled up from the chimneys of the village houses to be swiftly lost in the steadily falling snow. The ground cracked and crunched beneath them, a combination of snow, ice, and general muck from days of freezing cold and days of not-freezing cold, resulting in a wretched hazard.

Being the only mage-in-residence, charged with maintaining the half-hearted wards created long before his time, creating tonics and potions for the residents, casting spells for Bedros, and more, he was kept busy enough he rarely had time to leave the castle save to forage for the ingredients needed to make his inks. It made his few trips into the village all the more enjoyable. Often he went alone, but more than once he had accompanied Nerek on shared errands.

They were friends, after a fashion—if a man with whom he constantly argued, a man who drove him crazy, and whom he frequently wanted to throttle, could be considered a friend.

Today, however, the air was filled with more tension than snow. Nerek was well and truly mad at him, something which had not happened since Kohar's arrival, when he hadn't been amused to be barked at by an unkempt soldier with a gross lack of manners, and Nerek had not been pleased to learn he was going to have to work with some soft, spoiled city boy.

It had taken a few months for them to learn to cooperate, and even longer for it to not feel forced.

Suddenly being back where they started left Kohar feeling far more miserable than he would have expected, and the awful silence dragged interminably on.

There was also his damnable head, which only continued to throb and torment. Tired of the quiet, and desperate for distraction, Kohar asked, "So do you think this errant soldier is likely to be the rat?"

Nerek shook his head. "No. She's young and stupid and obviously infatuated and lust-addled…" He shot Kohar a nasty glare. "But I cannot seem her being part of this. If she is, it's probably against her will—blackmail or some such. We'll know for certain soon enough."

Kohar attempted to keep a rein on his own temper. "I am tired of you insinuating that I am putting a personal flirtation ahead of trying to save lives. I assure you I'm not. Your cousin simply has the worst possible timing in deciding to finally notice me."

"Whatever," Nerek snapped. "I'm just tired of seeing him trying to paw you every time you're in the same room, especially when there are still dead bodies in it, like this morning."

"Fair enough, but stop taking my head off for it, because I am not the one instigating the encount—"

"But you are the one looking at him like a moon-addled milksop!" Nerek practically bellowed, cheeks flushed with anger. "Could you please save your flirtations for after my men stop dying?"

"I have no control over your cousin, but I'll do my best to make him stop, since apparently you're incapable of speaking to him and instead have to blame me for everything," Kohar snarled right back.

"Fine," Nerek said.

"Fine," Kohar repeated bitingly.

By the time they reached the village, Kohar wanted to scream. Or push Nerek off his horse and leave him there on the ground to freeze to death. Stifling a sigh, Kohar hailed the first villager he saw, dismounting to better speak with her.

The local baker was a large, looming woman who wouldn't hurt a fly, unless that fly got into her dough. "Greetings," Kohar said with a smile, and exchanged pleasantries for several minutes before finally inquiring after the missing soldier.

"Don't know nothing about that," the woman replied. "Castle folk come and go as they please, we couldn't keep track of 'em even if we wanted to."

"Thank you for your time." Kohar mounted his

horse again, bid her good day, and followed a scowling Nerek off further into the village.

It took them three hours of asking and searching before the village chief could be bothered to bestir herself from her breakfast and escort them to a ramshackle hut a few miles south of the village belonging to a shepherdess known for generally keeping to herself, but who apparently hadn't been able to resist Corporal White's wiles.

Grumbling, wishing desperately for his bed or a hot meal, Kohar gladly left Nerek to do all the socializing with their officious escort. Left mercifully to his own devices, minus the occasional poisonous look from Nerek for being abandoned to a chatty person, Kohar mentally went over the inks he would be making, all the steps entailed—and the writing he would be doing through the night and well into morning.

They hadn't even reached the cabin when they came upon a woman sobbing hysterically, who shrieked when she saw the chief and started shouting about a dead woman, it wasn't her fault, she didn't know what happened.

Kohar shared a look with Nerek. Leaving the chief to handle the woman, they rode as swiftly as they safely could to the cabin. Reaching it, Nerek dismounted almost before his horse had come to a halt and strode to the door, throwing it open so hard Kohar was amazed it didn't fall off its hinges.

He stood in the open doorway, and after a moment beckoned Kohar to join him, face grim. The cabin was small, just one room, with a lean-to on the right side for storing food. On the rough-hewn bed, sprawled across a sheep-skin blanket, was a woman who had died in the middle of what should have been a good dream.

Kohar didn't want to think about what the poor lover must have thought, teasing a dreaming lover, thinking she would wake any moment, only…

"When I find the rat responsible, I am going to tear them limb from limb," Nerek said. "After I beat them half to death."

"Don't forget to force-feed them their own genitals—I liked that bit," Kohar replied. That almost got him a smile. The shadows in Nerek's eyes eased at least, which was all Kohar had hoped for. "What do we do now?"

"I'll send some men to recover the body. Let's speak with the woman, see if by some miracle she can tell us anything useful."

Kohar sighed. "If she snuck out early, before even I was awake, the number of people she encountered must have been limited."

"No one could, or would, say exactly when she left, but her shift ended at midnight. She likely snuck out almost immediately after. Solla arrived not long after that; I'll have to ask him when we get back if he saw something on his way in."

Back in the village, he left Nerek to go speak with the poor shepherd woman while he gathered the components he needed.

His first stop was Madame Karen, who was displeased he didn't come bearing her spell—until he explained why he was there. In short order, he had every component she could provide, and a direction to get the one she didn't.

That direction was back to the village baker, and then the blacksmith, where Kohar didn't bother to ask why a humble village blacksmith was keeping something as dangerous as powdered dragon poppy around. He paid for the three measures of it he needed, promised to forget the entire exchange, and headed back across the village to the chief's house.

Nerek was already waiting for him outside, stroking the nose of his horse and murmuring softly to it, face drawn, shoulders sagging. A sudden urge to go and hug him, reassure him, washed over Kohar. Was he losing his mind? He shook the strange impulse off—Nerek would likely clobber him even if he did try it—and made certain to approach noisily.

Stepping back from his horse and setting his shoulders once more, Nerek looked up at him. "Get what you need?"

"Enough for one spell, anyway," Kohar said. "As feared, I can't get what I need for the expelling part, but we'll worry about that later. What did the woman have to say?"

Nerek swung up into his saddle. "Not much, unfortunately. White arrived around two in the morning, give or take, and they had a small meal, enjoyed themselves in bed, then fell asleep. The woman woke up a few hours later, and…well, you can extrapolate the rest."

"Did she meet anyone on the road?"

"Not that she bothered to mention to her lover," Nerek said with a sigh. "I suppose that would be too easy. Come on, let's go home. There's nothing more to learn here."

Silently and swiftly they made the long trek back to the castle.

They were only a mile or so from it when a soldier came rushing toward them, breathless and frantic. "Captain! Captain! Another is dead! One of the stable hands this time."

"What?" Nerek roared. "Everyone was ordered to stay awake at all costs, who in the Regions dared to disobey me?"

The soldier swallowed but did not cower away

from his furious captain. "We don't know, sir. Don't think he meant to…"

Kohar swore loudly, barely noticing he used the exact same tone and phrasing as Nerek. They shared a look. "Come on," Nerek said sharply, breaking into his thoughts, kicking his horse into a gallop.

Kohar promptly did the same, the soldier who had come to find them close on their heels.

When they reached the castle a short time later, Kohar threw himself off his horse and tossed the reins at whomever was standing nearest, then bolted into the keep and through the halls to his chambers. Swinging a cauldron of water over the fire, he dumped the items in his satchel onto his work table, swept it clear of the other projects he'd been working on, and gathered the remaining components he would need.

Once he had all the components laid out, he set to work preparing them. Most of the powdered ones needed only to be turned into pastes so they'd blend more easily when he added them to the water. Others, like the della weed and heart-of-sun, needed to be cooked down in his table cauldron and then turned into paste.

Nerek appeared briefly in the midst of his work to tell him two more had died.

"I'm hurrying as best I can."

"I know."

They shared an agonized silence, and then each got back to work.

He'd just finished setting the ink aside to cool before he added the final two components and then bottled it when the sound of his door opening drew him again.

He looked up again and smiled tiredly at Solla, wondering why he felt disappointment instead of excitement.

"You have been in here for hours," Solla said, frowning. "Have you made any progress?"

Kohar nodded. "Yes, the ink is nearly ready. Once it's done, all I have to do is write the spell." He took a swallow of the stale tea he'd prepared and then forgotten about at some point.

"I'm sorry I can't be of more help to you and Nerek."

"It's not your problem to attend," Kohar replied, biting back that there was plenty Solla could be doing—helping keep people awake, helping Nerek question people, helping the distraught staff. Instead he did nothing, and didn't seem terribly sorry about it, whatever his words.

"Mm," Solla murmured noncommittally. He reached out and gently pushed back bits of hair which had come loose to fall across Kohar's cheeks, stroking his skin gently, fingers lingering on his cheekbone before finally pulling away. "It is a shame that all this trouble colors my visit, and that Nerek is being his usual self."

The earlier fight with Nerek came back to Kohar in full, and how frustrating that he agreed wholly with Nerek: this was the wrong time for Solla to be doing this. Why now, of all times, was Solla showing an interest in him?

And why, for the love of all the Regions, was he not enjoying it the way he'd always thought he would? Instead he just wanted to smack him for being so rude about Nerek—his cousin and captain of the soldiers who comprised the vast majority of the dead.

"Nerek's people are dying, and now staff we've known for as long as we've been here. I think his behavior is understandable."

"I suppose there is that…thankfully he has you to help him, though I doubt he appreciates that." His gaze dropped to Kohar's mouth. "I am told you come highly praised by those who know the ways of magic. Very highly praised."

"I just want to be good at what I do, same as most," Kohar said quietly, turning away—only to be yanked back and forcefully kissed. He tried to pull away, but Solla held him fast.

The sound of the door opening made Solla finally release him, and Kohar glared at him a moment before turning to see Nerek glaring at them. Not a glare, no…that expression was far too icy and cold to be a glare. His eyes were as bitter and hard as winter.

He was holding a tray of food and cider.

Without a word, Nerek set the tray on the table by the door, then turned and left, the door slamming shut behind him.

"I need to get back to work," Kohar snapped. "You should go."

"Of course," Solla murmured. "Perhaps we can speak again later."

Nodding reflexively as he turned away, Kohar fussed with his ink until the door mercifully opened and closed behind him. His stomach churned, remembering the look on Nerek's face. Had he just ruined their tenuous friendship with Solla's ill-timed attempts at flirting?

He scrubbed at his mouth, banishing the lingering feel of Solla's lips. How could he have wanted the man for years, practically since his arrival when they'd first met during a rainstorm or something, only to now feel increasing dread?

And how disappointing to find out the man was an appalling kisser. If that was how he treated women, maybe he'd had no choice but to start trying men. Kohar snorted a weak laugh and set to work on his ink, pulling the cooled cauldron and last set of components close.

Work, however, quickly became impossible, as he fought yawn after yawn, and his vision grew increasingly unfocused. What was wrong with him? Surely he shouldn't be this tired? He rubbed his eyes and then looked around for his tea. Hopefully an extra-strong cup would take the edge off and let him get this done.

He'd just set it to brewing when his door opened again, and his heart trip-trapped as he turned—and disappointment crashed over him as he saw not Nerek but Bedros.

Who chuckled and gave him a look Kohar didn't entirely understand. "Sorry I'm not Nerek, though I came about him. What in the Regions did you do to set him off? I finally had to order him to his office. It's bad enough we've got a demon running around this place, I don't need Nerek killing people as well."

Kohar made a face and tersely explained what had happened.

"Poor Nerek," Bedros said when he was done, sighing. "Well, I'll let the two of you work that out, though if my opinion matters at all, Kohar, you are better off rid of your silly infatuation."

As much as Kohar hated to admit it, he agreed. Solla's pretty face was proving to be the only interesting thing about him, and even that seemed less appealing by the minute, with the memory of Nerek's cold expression and the horrid kiss still fresh in his mind.

Regions, he was making no sense to himself anymore. Sighing, he turned back to finish making his tea, fighting yet another bone-cracking yawn.

"What's the progress on your ink?"

"It just needs to cool enough for me to work with," Kohar replied. "If I try too soon, the ink will run instead of holding. But not much longer now. I've been looking over the spell to ensure I get all the little details right, and it's more apparent with each rune that only a mage of impressive skill could do this."

"So this errant monk is at least as good as you?"

"Better. Much better. If the situation wasn't so dire, I wouldn't even be attempting the spells I'm about to write. I would love to know what my brother did to this mystery monk that he's decided to exact revenge by killing a bunch of people he's never even seen, who live months away and have nothing to do with anything."

"Sounds like a lovers' quarrel, if you ask me," Bedros said. "Love scorned, and all that. Immaterial, in the end. We don't need to know why—we just need to stop it."

Kohar set down his tea and stood to go check the ink—and dropped right back down as a wave of dizziness overtook him, followed by an exhaustion so heavy, it was all he could do to stay awake. "Something is wrong with me." He reached up as another wave of exhaustion and dizziness struck him—and felt something on his cheek, foreign and familiar all at once.

A stone dropped into his stomach as he pulled his fingers away and rubbed them together, slick, warm wax spreading from his thumb, which had touched his cheek, to the rest of his fingers. He pulled out his monocle with his other hand, which trembled faintly, and held it to his eye. The dregs of magic gleamed, and another stone joined the first in his gut.

Nearby, Bedros had gone still. "What's wrong?"

"Rune wax," Kohar said, and bolted across the room to where he kept emergency tonics, ripping the wax-sealed top off and guzzling it down, hoping it would counter the worst of the sleeping spell that had been woven into the whole mess. Damn it to the

Regions, he should have thought of that!

"Who in the Regions put it there?" Bedros asked.

Fury coiled through Kohar. "Solla is the only one who's touched me bare skin to bare skin today. That cretin." The hot anger turned abruptly to cold fear as a new realization struck. "Nerek. If he's tried to get me, he'll try to get to Nerek. He must have realized that with my making the ink, his time had run out, so he's finishing the job."

Not waiting for Bedros's reply, he threw open the library door and ran as fast as he could down the hall, pushing the door open and bolting down the stairs, nearly slipping several times, then onward to the armory. He shoved startled soldiers from his path, screaming Nerek's name, until he finally reached Nerek's office.

Practically kicking the damn door open, he bolted inside—and stopped in horror as he saw Nerek fast asleep, slumped over at his desk. Shoving his monocle into place, Kohar sought out the mark—there, on Nerek's hand. He strode across the room and used his tunic to wipe it off, then tried to shake Nerek awake.

No good. Kohar forced him to sit up, then tried slapping him. Then punching. All that got him was a sore hand. Ugh, he always forgot just how much it hurt to punch someone.

Damn it, there must be some way to save Nerek. There had to be. "You stupid bastard! I'll kill you myself if you let a stupid demon get the better of you!"

Looking frantically around, his eyes lighted upon fireplace—more specifically, the poker propped against it. Nerek would kill him—but at least Nerek would be alive to kill him.

Grabbing it up, he thrust the poker into the fireplace and willed it to heat up quickly. When he could not bear to stand still any longer, he turned around and strode back to the sleeping Nerek. Not giving himself time to think about it, he held the hot poker to Nerek's side.

After a moment that seemed to last an eternity, Nerek woke with a scream, jerking hard enough he tipped his chair backwards, crashing to the floor, swearing and trying to hold both his head and his side while struggling to stand

"You stupid bastard!" Kohar said, pounding on his chest. "I can't believe you fell asleep! I'm going to throw you in the fireplace! You stupid, stupid, stupid—"

"Yes, I get it," Nerek said, grabbing his wrists and forcing him to still. "What's going on? Why are you trying to burn me alive?"

"You fell asleep! Your stupid, backstabbing, cretin of a cousin is the one who's been putting the runes on people."

Nerek's eyes widened, then narrowed, and his face turned even colder than it had when he'd walked in on Solla kissing Kohar. "I'm a fucking fool. I just assumed—" He let go of Kohar's wrists, stepped back, hands flexing and unflexing. "I'll kill him myself." He looked around the room, as though expecting Solla to appear for execution, then finally swept back to land on Kohar. "Are you all right? Did he get you?"

"Oh, he got me all right," Kohar said bitterly. "That certainly explains why he's suddenly shown interest in me, why he forced that awful kiss on me."

"He what?" Nerek said, a look flickering over his face that Kohar didn't understand. "You…weren't kissing him by choice?"

"People are dying, of course I wasn't kissing him by choice!" Kohar bellowed. "I told you before, I have been doing nothing but trying to focus on this problem. He's the one who keeps pressing me. All because he apparently had a job to do." He raked back his hair, which must have come loose when he was running madly through the keep to save Nerek. "Figures the only person in this whole place who wants to kiss me really only wanted me dead."

"The only person—" Nerek cut off with a rough noise and several words Kohar couldn't understand, but were probably some choice crudities. "You're a damned fool, and after I've dealt with Solla, I'm dealing with you."

"What in the world did I do wrong?" Kohar demanded. "I just saved your—" The sentence turned into a startled yelp as Nerek yanked him in close, right up against that ridiculous chest, the leather armor uncomfortable but warm and solid. "Nerek?"

Nerek's reply was to kiss him. Kohar's eyes popped wide, lips parting with surprise, and Nerek took the opportunity to deepen the kiss.

Which was nothing at all like Solla's sad attempt. No, this was a *kiss*. Kohar had no idea what was going on, except that it seemed like the most natural thing in the world to throw his arms around Nerek's neck and kiss him back full measure.

His mouth was hot, consuming, the kiss as bossy and controlling as the rest of him, and damned if Kohar didn't like that. A lot.

Eventually, though, they had to draw apart. Reality crashed over him like snow falling from a roof. Nerek had kissed him.

Suddenly a whole lot of little things added up to a picture he really should have seen sooner.

"You're a dumbass," he finally managed.

"That's rich coming from you," Nerek retorted. He rubbed a gloved thumb over Kohar's lips, then with a rough noise stepped away. "I have to go find the bastard before he gets away with this. Update Bedros."

"Be careful," Kohar replied, mind still spinning with realizations and the burning memory of that kiss.

Looking entirely fed up with the world, Nerek stormed off. Kohar hastened to follow.

"Where is Solla?" Nerek barked as he reached the main hall of the barracks.

"He left right after he came out of your office, said you were sending him to investigate something to do with the demon. Must be nearly an hour ago by now."

Nerek's bellow of rage echoed through the hall, and every soldier in the room rose and stood at attention, absorbing his anger and worry and making it their own. Like they always did, because they would follow Nerek into the darkest Regions. "Where did he go?"

"Across the border," said a guard from the farthest corner of the room. "I saw him when I was on watch, but when I asked they said he'd gone on your orders."

Cursing, Nerek ordered the soldiers to follow him and headed off, likely bound for the stables.

Kohar headed back to the main keep, where Bedros was sitting at a table by the fire, eating slowly as he went about the grim work of filling out and signing death certificates for all the soldiers and servants Solla had killed.

He looked up at the sound of footsteps. "Nerek?"

"Alive."

"Thank the gods," Bedros said, and looked for a moment like he might actually cry from relief. He set his quill aside and sat up straight. "So what's going on now?"

"He went after Solla, who is trying to flee across

the border. Hopefully he'll manage it, though I don't know if he'll bring Solla back dead or alive."

Bedros lifted one shoulder. "Either is fine, frankly. Dead would be cheaper. Alive would be less paperwork. Are you both all right?"

"Fine," Kohar said quietly, and sat when Bedros motioned he should. "How long have I been blithely unaware of Nerek's feelings?"

Bedros let out a sharp laugh. "Finally got there did you? Did he say something?"

"After a fashion." Kohar didn't touch his fingers to his lips, but only barely. In between the frets about Solla, the horrible weather Nerek and his soldiers were fighting to get to the backstabbing bastard, his thoughts flitted around that kiss. Just how badly he wanted another.

Soft chuckles drew him from his thoughts. "Well, I'm happy the two of you have finally sorted that out. Another month of tension and obliviousness and I was going to lock the two of you in the pantry until some sort of resolution was achieved."

Kohar rolled his eyes. "I'm guessing I made my fancy new ink for nothing. I'll do the spell anyway to be sure, but if I had to guess, I'd say he destroyed the remaining runes he had, and without another one to jump to, the demon is gone."

"Well, I'm sorry you wasted all that time and effort, but I prefer this to having to locate, trap, and expel a demon."

"Agreed."

"Eat something before you fall over, Kohar." Bedros shoved the plate of food he'd been ignoring across the table, and Kohar took it gladly, too exhausted and hungry to argue over propriety and other stupid rules.

The wait was agonizing. Kohar went back to his

room to try and work on the spell, but after he screwed up three times on just the first line, gave up entirely and returned to the great hall to wait with Bedros.

That just got him a smirk. "He'll be fine."

"I know," Kohar said irritably. "I'm not fretting over Nerek."

"Uh huh. So who kisses better: Nerek or Solla?"

Kohar gave him a withering look and didn't reply.

Bedros just snickered.

"Rider!"

The guard's voice cut through the castle, and everyone went still from surprise for a moment.

Then they all rushed to the courtyard as Bedros called for the gates to be opened.

Who in the world would be coming to see them at this hour? Was it one of Nerek's soldiers, was something wrong? Were they on their way back and this was just the scout?

He watched, shivering in the cold, as the man dismounted clumsily, probably from being half frozen. Then the man threw back his hood and looked around, and Kohar gaped a moment before racing across the ward. "Taniel, what in the Regions are you doing here?" He grabbed Taniel's shoulders, shook him hard, and then pulled him into a hug.

"Did you not get my letter?"

"Of course I got your letter, though it hasn't done much good in the end."

Taniel's face fell. "What do you mean?"

"Inside, inside," Kohar replied, and they all fled back into the relative warmth of the keep. Once they were settled by the fire, and reasonably thawed, he related all that had transpired over the past day.

"I'm so sorry," Taniel said as he finished. "I had hoped my letter would reach you in time, since there was no way I would be able to in this stupid weather."

"It's not your fault."

"But it is," Taniel replied, looking near to tears. "All of this is my stupid fault. I never should have—" He broke off and stared glumly at his hands, looking worn and broken.

"Never should have what?" Kohar asked. "Tell us the whole story, Tani."

Taniel sighed and accepted the cup of cider a servant handed him. After several swallows, he finally started speaking. "His name is Vosgi. He and I were…close." Taniel's frown deepened, bitterness and exhaustion washing over him. "We both have the licenses to do high level magic. Vosgi wanted to go even further. To my shame, I helped him with some of the earliest experiments because I admit I liked the thrill of doing magic nobody else in the country had ever managed. But Vosgi…he kept going, moved into the darker stuff. I begged him to stop. He wouldn't listen. I finally confessed everything to our superiors. I was cast out, but Vosgi… Vosgi resisted, killed people trying to escape." His hand went to his side reflexively, the way Nerek's did when some of his old wounds acted up.

Kohar pursed his lips at the gesture but let it go for the moment.

"They finally caught him, imprisoned him, and I thought that would be the end of the matter. I was packing my things when he escaped, killing still more people. I wrote the letter to you, then headed here as quickly as I could. But injury and weather held me back, and I guess Vosgi managed to get here well ahead of me."

"Injury? Are you all right now? What happened? What did that bastard do? Do you need healing? When did you last rest?" Kohar demanded.

Taniel chuckled and smiled fondly. "Still a hundred questions at once with you, Kohi. He stabbed me, but not well. Then on our travels my horse slipped, threw me, cost me a broken arm. I had to remain in camp while it healed. After that, it was snow, snow, and more snow." He sighed and finished his cider.

Kohar immediately swapped his full cup for Taniel's empty one and cast him a warning look when he tried to protest.

Into the silence, Bedros said, "Pardon me if I'm pointing out something awkward, but is there a reason you two look nothing alike? If you'd not told me you were brothers, I never would have thought you were related."

Kohar and Taniel laughed, and Kohar said, "He's adopted. He was abandoned as a child, we think. My parents found him on the streets, just days from death, and took him in. By the time he was all healed up, they couldn't bear to part with him."

Taniel gave him a look, but Kohar ignored it. If he wanted to share the full, actual story of how he'd come to join their family, he could later. For now, the simplified version their parents had always gone with would suffice.

"I'm glad you found a happy home," Bedros said. "Your hair is beautiful. I've never seen such a perfect shade of gold."

"Thank you," Taniel said, reaching up to touch where it was still bound up in a tidy bun, secured with a plain, wooden hair stick. "The monks wanted me to cut it off, but I never completed my vows, so they couldn't make me yet. I never really was cut out for the life; I just wanted to study the magic." He set the cider aside, and his hand curled into his fist in his lap. "I'm so sorry. This is all my fault—"

"No," Bedros said, in a commanding tone

Kohar rarely heard—the voice of a duke, a lord of the realm, master of the castle. "The only one to blame here is this contemptible Vosgi who is lashing out like a petulant, spoiled child who didn't get his way. You did the right thing in confessing, turning both of you in, knowing it would cost you dearly. He is the only one to blame for his actions. Do not take on his guilt; that's not your burden to carry."

Taniel stared at him a moment, then gave a jerky nod. "Thank you, Your Grace."

"Bah. Everyone may as well call me Bedros. It's not as though we really stand much on ceremony around this old place. Nerek and Kohar are more the lords of the keep than me. I just do the paperwork and the taxes."

"Ugh, taxes." Kohar wrinkled his nose. "I really wish—"

"Riders!"

He rose and dashed across the hall to the doors, where guards barely got them open in time to avoid his crashing right into them.

Outside, coming into the ward just as the lamplighters were finishing up the torches there, Nerek came in at the head of a group of ten soldiers—four of them securing a bruised and battered Solla.

"You caught him!" Kohar said. "Ha! I knew the bastard wouldn't be able to escape you!"

Nerek seemed startled, and then pleased, by the words, smiling briefly at Kohar before he once more became all business. "Your Grace, I've captured the fiend responsible for murdering our people. He has been thoroughly searched for any remaining magical items, though I advise our mage-in-residence look him over as well. Are you going to leave him to a justiciar or take care of the matter yourself?"

"I haven't decided yet. Lock him up and make

sure he can't do anything stupid or dangerous. Did he have anything to say in his defense?"

"Nothing worth repeating," Nerek said, and jerked his head at the soldiers who had Solla secured.

Kohar scowled as they passed by. "I don't suppose I could persuade someone to punch him for me?"

Nerek gave him an amused look. "You could punch him yourself."

"Ugh, no. I tried punching you to wake you up," Kohar replied, shaking his poor hand. "My knuckles still hurt. I'll leave it to you soldiers."

Nerek rolled his eyes but then spun neatly on his heel and delivered a punch to Solla's jaw that sent him tumbling to the floor with a cry of pain. Turning back, Nerek lifted a brow at Kohar. "Will that suffice?"

"Oh, yes, that was lovely," Kohar replied, then smiled in a way he hadn't bothered to in years because there'd never been anyone he thought he could flirt with. "I'll thank you for it later."

Of all the reactions he'd expected, Nerek's cheeks turning pink was nowhere near the list. "Shut up, mage," he groused as he stormed off, his soldiers gaping and then muffling laughter in their heavy winter gloves as they hauled Solla back to his feet and dragged him away.

Taniel snickered. "I see you and your soldier finally got together."

"Did everyone know except me?" Kohar asked.

"Yes," Bedros, Taniel, and the remaining soldiers and servants replied.

Throwing up his arms, Kohar said, "I'm going to go make certain the prisoner is secured from a magical standpoint. Taniel, pick a bedroom."

He made his way briskly to his room first, where he pulled out spells he'd prepared not long after his arrival, and then had almost never needed. Tucking them into one of the pouches at his waist, he gathered everything else he would need and then headed back to the main keep and down the stairs to the cellar and dungeons.

At the very back, in the only cell that didn't have a small window for air and light, Solla sat against the wall on a threadbare sleeping roll, arms folded on his bent knees. His smile was cold and derisive as he saw Kohar. "My cousin's little darling. Seducing you was pathetically easy."

"I really wouldn't be so sure of that," Kohar replied, then pulled out the scrolls he'd carefully tucked away. Unrolling the first one, slightly larger than his hand, he braced it on the tablet he'd brought, securing it with the wood slats on each side so it would lay flat. Then he pulled out a quill and bottle of ink and wrote in the last few runes. As the spell shimmered to life, he placed his hand on it, spoke a few words of transfer, then extended his hand outward and finished the transfer spell.

The magic struck Solla, who gasped and swore, clawing at his throat—and then gave up, settling for a hateful glare since he would not be doing any talking for several days, at which point Kohar would decide whether or not to renew the spell.

Pulling out the next scroll, now that he could work in peace, he cast a spell that checked thoroughly for the presence of magic on an item or person. When that turned up nothing, he cast a collaring spell that further bound Solla to his cell. If he tried to escape, he'd simply pass out.

"You're lucky Nerek didn't simply slit your throat and leave your body to freeze and then rot in the spring thaw," Kohar replied. "Enjoy your stay."

He turned and left, and headed back outside

once more and across the ward and around the side to the armory and barracks, where he assumed Nerek had gone.

But when he reached Nerek's room, it was to find it empty. "Where's he gone?" he asked the aide who came in with a tray of food.

"I saw him with the soldiers, preparing the bodies for the pyres."

"Of course," Kohar replied, and motioned for the boy to go.

At loose ends, as there was no way he was trekking back into that abysmal cold yet again, he looked over his choices and finally took a seat on the edge of Nerek's bed. Strictly speaking, Nerek had a room in the main keep that was a proper suite befitting his rank. But much like Kohar, he preferred to sleep where he worked, so he was always near to hand for emergencies.

The crackle of the fire, the familiar muffled chaos of the armory, soon had him yawning again. Stupid Nerek had better hurry back, or Kohar would just…

*~*~*

"Wake up!"

"Fuck you," Kohar grumbled, and tried to bury his head in the blankets again.

"This is not your bed!"

"It is now." Shoving away the hand on his shoulder, Kohar turned over, yanked the blankets back up, and tried to get warm again.

There was muttering and sighing, more cold air as someone yanked his boots off and messed with his belt, nearly waking him completely. But then everything stilled again, mercifully, though he could still hear distant muttering and grumbling. Had he left something burning and annoyed a servant again? He didn't care.

The bedding lifted again, letting in cold air, and Kohar cringed and whined. He was spared having to wake up and commit murder, however, by the addition of a sudden furnace to the bed. That was more like it. Turning back around, Kohar cuddled up to all the delightful, winter-banishing warmth and sunk back into sleep, chased by the sound of somebody saying his name on a long-suffering sigh.

Kohar woke overheated and with light bathing his face, neither of which was usually something he faced first thing in the morning. He stared blankly up at an unfamiliar window and ceiling. It was the clash and bang from outside that finally brought comprehension. "Why in the Regions am I sleeping in the armory?"

"You tell me."

Kohar yelped and sat up, shoving his hair out of his face, swearing when it promptly disobeyed him, and wrestling with it for a couple of minutes before he was finally able to scowl properly at Nerek. "Must you?"

"Yes," Nerek replied. "You're the one who tried to steal my bed."

"Oh, right. I was waiting for you. Why was I waiting for you?"

"I assume it had something to do with the vindictive muting of my prisoner. Not a criticism, mind. Usually you're the nice one, though."

Kohar swung his legs over the edge of the bed, noting absently someone had removed his boots and belt. "Sorry, I didn't actually mean to steal your bed. I hope I didn't put you on the floor or something."

"No, I was not getting kicked out of my own damned bed," Nerek said, and damned if his cheeks didn't flush the barest bit. "Though I may have taken the floor if I'd known you were so clingy."

"I am not!"

"You are—" Nerek broke off. "I am not getting into such a stupid argument with you."

Kohar smiled. "We've had stupider. I think—" he stopped, then sighed as his stupid hair broke free of the bun he'd tried to secure it in, spilling all around and in his face. "I'm going to shave it off, I swear to the Regions."

"You wouldn't!" Nerek hastily stood. "Whatever. Hurry up and go back to your own room, so I can get some work done." He fled the room like he was being chased by a fire dragon, leaving Kohar gaping after him.

And then dissolving into laughter. Captain Tough-and-Scruffy was *shy*.

Smirking, Kohar gave up on his hair and focused on righting his clothes and scrounging up his boots. He was just about to leave when he spied a familiar hair comb lying on Nerek's desk. So he must have found it in the snow or the halls or wherever Kohar had lost it.

Twisting his hair and jamming the comb into place, Kohar departed Nerek's room and headed back through the armory—ignoring the looks and smirks of the soldiers he passed.

"Have fun last night, Master Mage?" one finally called out.

"No," Kohar replied coolly. "Not with His Grace signing death warrants, the good Captain arresting his own cousin, and pyres I must set this evening to put our comrades upon. I fell asleep waiting to give a report. What did you think we were doing? Celebrating death and betrayal?"

Face red with shame, everyone around him looking little better, the soldier mumbled an apology and scuttled off.

Kohar continued on his way, returning quickly to his room to clean up and put on fresh clothes.

Then he went to get some breakfast before he set to work on the pyres so they'd be ready that evening.

He worked on the roof, a special pavilion at the back end of the castle meant for ceremonies and funeral pyres, since level ground was as hard to find there as a warm day. First he cast spells that would keep the area clear of snow for several hours. Then he got a few soldiers to help him haul the platforms and other supplies up and get it all arranged.

Finally, he returned to his workroom to write out enough spells for the seven pyres.

Seven people. Five soldiers and two servants. All dead because his brother's ex-lover got mad at being caught doing something forbidden. Kohar sighed as he finished the first of the seven spells and set it aside to dry.

By the time he was done, he was stiff, sore, and ready to go back to bed. He'd have to settle for tea. Climbing to his feet with a groan, stretching to ease the worst of the aches, he shuffled over to his table and got a kettle heating, pouring the tea into a pot and then slumping right there on his stool, half-sprawled on the table as he waited.

A familiar banging came at his door, and then it swung immediately open, Nerek's form filling the doorway as his eyes swept the room—and finally landed on him. Some of the tightness around his eyes eased, and the barest hint of a smile flickered before he strode into the room like he had a thousand times before.

"If you're coming to give me work to do, go away," Kohar mumbled. "I'm finished with work for the day."

Nerek came up to the table but remained on the opposite side of it. "I came to see how you were doing, since no one has seen much of you today, not even the cooks, despite the fact they're making dragon stew."

Kohar perked up at that. "They are?"

"Yes," Nerek said, rolling his eyes. "I take it you've been busy with spells for tonight?"

"Yes. They're finished, more or less." Kohar yawned and rubbed his eyes. "I just need to stay awake long enough to cast them." Funeral pyres were always set with magic, since they could burn in any weather, burn hot enough that nothing survived the pyre, but the heat was contained so that people were not forced to keep a great distance between them and the flames. Magic fire was expensive, and difficult, but there were perks to working for a duke who kept a mage-in-residence and cared about his people enough to ensure they received such things. "Have you had a chance to meet my brother?"

Nerek gave him a look. "It would be hard not to—everyone is talking about him, and he's become fast friends with His Grace."

"That's a terrible idea. Who let that happen?"

"You," Nerek retorted.

"I'm busy!"

"Looked like you were sleeping to me."

Kohar slid from his stool and rounded the table. "Did you just come see me to be aggravating, or did you have some other purpose?"

"I told you why I came to see you." Nerek folded his arms across his chest and scowled. "Why must you always be such a brat?"

"This brat saved your life."

"Only because you probably wanted to save the pleasure of killing me for yourself."

Kohar laughed and rested his hands on his hips. "Are you going to keep standing there blustering, you clod-head, or are you going to kiss me?"

"Gods save me from obnoxious mages," Nerek said, but then Kohar was the one up against the table, his arms full of voracious, scruffy soldier, and a hot mouth doing more to wake him up than any cup of tea ever could.

Regions, if he'd known Nerek could kiss like this, he'd have flirted with the man sooner. Maybe. He'd always been really good at missing the obvious when it came to things like this. Without his siblings to tell him he was being flirted with, Kohar had always missed it.

He moaned into the kiss, enjoying how consuming Nerek was, the way he demanded all of Kohar's attention and would not accept anything less. His stubble was going to leave Kohar's face red, and his mouth would probably ache by the time they were done, but oh would it all be worth it.

When they finally parted, he was panting for breath and utterly, completely, hopelessly lost in those green eyes. "How long have you wanted me, Nerek? Why in the Regions didn't you say something sooner?"

"You wanted him," Nerek said sourly, letting him go, eyes sliding away. "All you ever do with me is complain and argue. Every time he's around, you take pains to look even more beautiful than usual, but you really don't care when I stroll into your damn room and see you in your bed clothes or whatnot. How in the Regions was I supposed to say anything?"

Kohar opened his mouth, then closed it again. It was true. He never fretted when Nerek was around—he never had to fret. "It's ability you admire, not appearance. What good would dressing up have done when I was trying to prove myself? And then I just got used to not having to pretend or fuss with you." He stopped, stared. "You think I'm beautiful?"

"No, I think you're hideous, that's why I'm here kissing you and making a fool of myself when I have five hundred other things that need doing."

He pulled away, but Kohar grabbed his arm and managed to reel him back in. "Stop being grumpy and get back to kissing me. We're not going to inspire more rumors if you behave."

"Shut up," Nerek said with a sigh. "You're so annoying. You make me insane. You're a spoiled brat who stole my bed, my blankets, and nearly smothered me with your clinging."

"I'll make it up to you by being way more fun the next time I'm in your bed," Kohar replied, and dragged him into another of those delightful kisses. "Where did a grouch like you learn to kiss like that?" Nerek just kissed him again, until Kohar's lips were sore and he needed badly to breathe. "Seriously, how did you acquire such skill?"

Nerek groaned and shoved away from where he'd pinned Kohar to the table. "That's a stupid question and I'm not answering it."

"You're blushing!"

"Shut up," Nerek hissed. "You are making me regret me this."

"This what? This kiss? This admitting you like me? This—"

"This letting you live when I should have tossed

you out in the snow right from the start," Nerek snapped. "I may yet do it."

Kohar grinned. "If you killed me, you wouldn't get to see me naked in your bed."

Nerek covered his eyes with the heels of his hands. "I hate you. And no, we are not doing anything in my bed. The rumors are already out of control after last night and your little reprimand this morning." He dropped his hands to scowl. "The very last thing I need is a barracks full of my people hearing things. I would never get any peace."

Oh, that was too easy. Why had he never thought to flirt with Nerek before? It was already his new favorite thing to do. Batting his eyes as ridiculously as possible, Kohar said, "Why, Captain, are you saying you're going to make me scream?"

"Stop that," Nerek hissed. "I had no idea you could be this much of a brat."

Kohar laughed and threw his arms around Nerek's neck, laughing harder when Nerek tried to push him away. "Have you always been this easy to fluster?"

"You know damn good and well that I do not tolerate nonsense."

"And yet you want me," Kohar replied. "Anyway, it's not nonsense. It's called flirting. Surely people have flirted with you before."

"My mother is an unbending, humorless general who thinks I'm soft and weak and an embarrassment to her good name. They call her General Stoneheart behind her back. Do you really think people flirted with me?"

Kohar kissed him softly, angry at a woman he would probably never meet, hurting for the boy who was never allowed to play and flirt and have fun. "Well, I'm flirting with you. It's much more fun than flirting with customers in the hopes of good tips."

Heavy hands settled at his hips, and then he was being treated to another one of those divine, rough and hungry kisses. Why in the Regions had it never occurred to him to do this sooner? Why had he always dismissed the idea of Nerek as a lover? Past him was stupid.

Forcing himself to withdraw, though he did it slowly and thoroughly, eliciting an utterly delightful groan he wanted to hear again and again. "As much as I would love to drag you to my bed and ravish you until you can't move, we should probably get to dinner."

"Yes," Nerek said quietly, but gave a last soft, lingering kiss that left Kohar tingling.

"Seriously, where did you learn to kiss so well? Because I have kissed a lot of people—"

"Including my damned cousin."

Kohar rolled his eyes. "Yes, and he was absolutely awful. I was a better kisser my very first time, and let me tell you, the man who put up with me that night was a saint."

"Stop talking about kissing other people," Nerek groused, but his dark eyes gleamed with mirth. "If you really must know, I learned from the whores that followed my mother's camp. Women. Men. Both."

"Oh, the bashful Captain has some adventures to his name. Tell me more. What a pretty image, you caught between a woman and a man. What about two women? Two men?"

Nerek shoved him away with a groan and headed for the door. "Shut up! This is why I didn't want to tell you. I hate you."

"That is a lie," Kohar said, gathering up his spell scrolls and racing to catch up to him, latching onto his arm as they walked. Nerek gave him a look but didn't dislodge his hand, and if Kohar didn't know any better, he'd swear there was a hint of a smile there.

The great hall was already crowded when they entered, a hush sweeping over as they were spotted, followed by an immediate increase in chatter. Kohar rolled his eyes, but didn't drop his arm until they reached Bedros, who sat at the centermost long table, at the end closest to the fire. It had been strange, when Kohar had first arrived, to see a lord who did not have a fancy high table apart from the rest of the castle inhabitants. But it was the kind of strangeness that had made him like his new lord, even if his new home had been remote, desolate, and nothing at all like the vibrant city he'd left behind.

Sitting across from Bedros, next to his brother, Kohar ignored the smirking smirks they were both giving him. "Castle rumor is that you two are fast friends."

Bedros laughed. "We are the least interesting rumor in the castle."

Nerek scowled as he heaped his plate with food from the platters set down the length of the table. "I wish people worked half as hard as they gossip. What is there to talk about?"

"My Captain of the Guard finally getting through to my oblivious Mage-in-Residence, though of course you two pick the worst possible time. At least the matter is resolved, though I wish it had been resolved with fewer dead." With that, Bedros took up his cup of wine and stood. Lifting the cup high, he said, "To our fallen, gone too soon, taken unjustly. May their spirits return to the Great Hearth, and their memory live in the Guiding Winds eternally. To death, and to life."

Everyone chorused the final words, and Bedros tossed the wine in his cup into the fire before sitting again. "Kohar, you've barely touched your stew. Are you dying? Or distracted?"

"I've only just got here!"

Taniel snickered. "I see that hasn't changed. Aunt Merida could barely keep up with making it, you stole so much. There was hardly any for the customers."

"Ugh, go back to your monastery."

Nerek set his wine down, a positively evil smirk overtaking his face, a gleam in his eye. "Tell us more stories of Kohar as a boy. He mentioned flirting with customers?"

"Flirting? Taniel howled with laughter. "Flirting is the *least* he did with—"

"You will shut up right now!" Kohar said, and groaned as he was summarily ignored.

By the time dinner ended, he was determined to murder all three of them.

Those thoughts lapsed, however, as everyone filed out of the great hall and up the stairs to the pavilion. The levity of dinner faded to a somber mood as they gathered around the pyres. Kohar went to each one and cast the spells, rejoining Nerek and the others as the flames caught.

Bedros started the singing, and gradually everyone else joined in, the hymn of farewell sending their lost friends to their new home.

*~*~*

Kohar was bent over a new set of inks, two bottled and three still to go, when he heard his door open. "Get out, I'm not doing any more work today, I don't care if you're the lord of the manor."

"I'm not the lord of the manor, and I'm not here to work," Nerek said, the words punctuated by the closing and locking of the door.

Oh, that sounded promising. "Let me finish this."

"Take your time," Nerek replied, in a voice that made Kohar want to just let the ink rot. But making the full set had taken him two days, and he wasn't about to waste all that time and effort. Forcing himself to focus, he meticulously poured and capped the remaining inks, then went and put them all in their places on his desk.

When he was finally done, he turned and leaned against the desk, staring at Nerek, who lingered by the door still. "Well? Did you just come see me to stare?"

Nerek pushed lazily away from the wall and walked—prowled, mercy, that was distracting and arousing—toward him, green eyes like flames. "You've been wearing your hair down more."

Kohar resisted the urge to reach up and touch his hair, which he'd mostly left down, only pulling the front back so it wasn't in his way while he worked. "I have it on good authority that it's a particular weakness of the Captain of the Guard, and I've been trying to get him to notice me." They'd been so busy the past month, and respecting the period of mourning, that they'd done little more than exchange heated kisses and fall asleep together in whichever bed was closest. More and more, they used Kohar's chambers, since they afforded more privacy than Nerek's.

"An effective strategy," Nerek murmured as he reached Kohar, pinning him to the desk and feasting on his mouth, rough and bossy and still the best kisser Kohar had ever encountered. He tugged his hands free and wrapped them around Nerek's waist, delighting in the way he hadn't worn all his armor and weapons, though he probably still had a knife or two secreted somewhere.

He slid his hands down and pushed beneath Nerek's tunic to get his hands on that marvelous ass. Even when he'd been an oblivious nitwit he'd admired Nerek's backside.

Nerek broke the kiss, but only to work his mouth along Kohar's jaw and throat, making a frustrated noise when he reached fabric. "I hope you are amenable to missing dinner."

"I've gone to the kitchens late before," Kohar replied breathlessly. "Stop asking stupid questions and get to the part where you fuck me, Captain."

A rough, hungry noise tore from Nerek's throat, and then Kohar was being kissed ravenously again, eager hands setting to work on his belt. It was gone in a moment, and Nerek tore away to pull his tunic and under tunic off in an impressively smooth move. He skated a hand along Kohar's bare chest, and the heat and approval in his eyes was the most gratifying thing Kohar had seen in a long time—especially considering he was all squishy softness where Nerek was tight, trim muscle.

He got more kisses, more rough stubble scraping along his throat, nibbles at his collarbone and sucking bites at his nipples and down his chest. He was so hard it hurt, and standing was becoming increasingly difficult. "Bed," he managed, "and you're wearing more clothes than me."

Nerek pulled away like it cost him something and dragged him over to the bed set in a nook that was separated from the rest of the room by an archway and curtains that Kohar rarely bothered to close. "Get naked, mage."

Kohar obeyed, though he was distracted more than once by the sight of Nerek becoming increasingly naked. Regions, if he'd thought Nerek good looking before…

The man was practically a work of art, toned and fine, layers of muscle and fat that explained why he was always hotter than even the fire in the great hall, why he made even the most strenuous tasks look so effortlessly easy. And gods have mercy, not a single part of him was out of proportion.

"You're still dressed," a very naked Nerek said as he prowled closer, pushed Kohar onto the bed, and pulled off his hose and underclothes.

Kohar licked his lips, torn between lust for Nerek and the painful awareness that he was not nearly as impressive when the clothes were gone. "I'm starting to see why whores were more than happy to teach you things."

"I regret ever telling you about that," Nerek said, and practically tossed him further up into the bed, nearly causing him to knock against the headboard. "As though you've room to talk, *flirting* with customers instead of working."

"Excuse you, but occasionally prostituting myself right in front of my domineering aunt without her noticing took a lot of work."

"Shut up," Nerek said, spreading his legs and settling between them. Kohar moaned, letting his head fall back against the pillows, closing his eyes because otherwise he might come simply from the sight alone.

A hot, heavy hand rested on his chest and trailed slowly down, and Nerek's voice was rough and low, sending shivers down Kohar's spine. "I like you naked."

"I'm a pasty, pudgy mage," Kohar replied, dragging his eyes open, heartened by the heat in those too-green eyes. "But if that impresses you, far be it for me to complain."

In reply, Nerek leaned in to kiss him and wrapped one hand around his cock, causing Kohar to writhe and moan and stop caring what they were talking about. He wrapped arms around Nerek, holding him close, wanting him close always.

Pulling away just barely enough to speak, Nerek murmured, "You're beautiful." He squeezed

Kohar's cock, sending shudders through his body. "I've wanted to see you like this for years."

"You should have said something."

"How can you be so good at flirting with customers and so horrible at noticing when someone wants you?"

Kohar moaned as Nerek stroked him, his other hand reaching down to tease and fondle his sac. "Flirting is easy, and my siblings and cousins always pointed out when someone looked willing to pay me for special treatment in the back room. That's what I'm used to. Not handsome soldiers scowling and having jealous fits." Nerek's mouth worked his throat, his chest—and then he withdrew, making Kohar swear loudly and colorfully. "Why did you stop?"

"I have every intention of fucking you, and I wanted to get the oil before we got any further." His smirk said he also just liked to be a jerk, but that was hardly surprising.

Sitting up, Kohar shoved him down and scrambled off the bed, digging in a basket he kept on a nearby shelf for oil he hadn't bothered to use for weeks. Months? Didn't matter. He carried it back to the bed and shoved Nerek right back down when he tried to sit up, straddling those heavy thighs and slicking his fingers before wrapping them around that thick, heavy cock.

The look on Nerek's face, hungry and eager and happy, was one Kohar would remember forever. But he also couldn't help but mess with him. "So how do you compare to your imprisoned cousin?"

That got him exactly the annoyed look he'd been hoping for—and then he was sent wooshing back, pinned to the bed, all the breath knocked out of him, hands pinned above his head with one hand, Nerek's scowling face only a breath away from his. "You're not funny."

"Yes, I am," Kohar said with a delighted laugh, not-really-struggling against Nerek's delightfully strong grip. He batted his eyes. "So do you want to play whore and customer?"

"Shut up, shut up, shut up," Nerek said, and kissed him hard, leaving his mouth sore and throbbing. "You're such a brat. You're even worse now than you were before, and I didn't think that was possible."

"You like it, or you wouldn't still be hard." Kohar squirmed beneath him. "Come on, are you a paying customer or not? Get what you're paying for or why—" He yelped and laughed as that got him a sound swat on the thigh.

Then a hot, slick finger pushed inside him, and Kohar moaned loud and long. "Been a long time since anyone's done that."

"Oh? Here I thought you and Madame Karen had some sort of casual arrangement."

Kohar laughed, though it turned into another moan as Nerek demonstrated just how well the camp whores had instructed him. "Is that why you don't like her? But no, I've never been interested in women that way. I just make spells for her—including the occasional naughty one. We're mages, we talk about that kind of stuff."

Nerek huffed a soft laugh and added another finger, setting Kohar to moaning and begging.

"Please," he finally gasped out. "I can't take anymore. I want your cock."

He swore honest to gods fire flashed in Nerek's eyes as he withdrew his fingers and lined up his cock. "Do you know how long I've wanted to do this? To be right here, with you?"

"Well, next time speak—" the rest of the sentence was lost in a howl as Nerek thrust inside him, all at once, nothing held back. Wrists still pinned, Nerek's cock buried inside him, hopelessly tangled now in the mussed bedding he hadn't bothered to tidy that morning, the rest of the world ceased to exist. He never wanted to be anywhere else. Just there, pinned beneath Nerek and stuffed full, those green eyes looking at him like he was the whole world. "Move, already."

Nerek shifted his grip to hold one wrist in each hand, bracing himself as he pulled partly out and then thrust back in, setting up a torturous rhythm that left Kohar writhing and howling, moaning and begging, delightfully helpless as Nerek drove him to the brink of madness.

That rough, husky voice filled his ear. "Come on my cock, Kohar. Now."

Kohar really wanted to defy him, but he was absolutely incapable of resisting that voice giving such delightful orders. Screaming Nerek's name, he came, the world completely whiting out around him.

When he came back down, it was to Nerek still thrusting away, using his pliant, wrung-out body, making him whimper and moan. Nerek buried his face in Kohar's throat and came, sinking in deep and shuddering as his climax overtook him. He let go of Kohar's wrists, and Kohar held him close, enjoying the warmth and weight of him as they both slowly calmed down.

Eventually, though, he had to nudge Nerek off him. Rolling over to sprawl across that marvelous chest, stroking the lines of a horrible-looking scar, he said, "I suppose that was adequate."

Nerek rolled his eyes. "I'm going to start gagging you."

"Oh, so you want to play kidnapper and—"

"Stop it," Nerek hissed, cheeks flushing. "You're a horrible person. No, I do not want to roleplay anything!"

Kohar dissolved into laughter, muffling it poorly against Nerek's chest—and screeching when he got a solid smack to the ass. "Hey! I'm a nice boy from a good family. There will be no spanking before the fifth—" He kept laughing into the kiss, until Nerek rolled him into the bedding again and distracted him from making more teasing remarks.

When they had finally depleted all their energy, and Kohar had made them tea and fetched some of the food he kept in the room for when he was up before the kitchens, Nerek said, "This is exactly why I refuse to do anything in my room. I would never hear the end of it from my soldiers, and I get enough from you."

That just made Kohar grin. "You don't want the whole castle to know how loudly I scream when you fuck me or all the lewd jokes I make?"

"Funnily enough, no."

"So prim for a man who paid whores to give him lessons," Kohar said with a snicker.

"So improper for a man too dense to know when someone wants him," Nerek retorted.

Kohar's snickering faded into a soft smile. "Wish it hadn't taken a tragedy to bring us together, but I'm happy you finally said something and I finally noticed the right cousin. What do you think will become of him?"

"Execution," Nerek said flatly. "Bedros and I already signed off on it for the justiciar. Unless he finds reason to negate it, Solla die in the spring."

"I'm sorry."

Nerek shook his head. "He's the only one who should be sorry. Don't waste any more time on him. He chose his path." He stole Kohar's remaining cheese.

Finishing his tea, Kohar set all the dishes aside and snuggled beneath the blankets, eager to be away from the winter chill that overtaking him now he was cooled off from their exertions. "I wish you could have met my whole family. They would have liked you, happily taken you in as one of us. My mother would be pleased I settled down with someone so sensible; my father would have talked your ear off about his soldiering days before he returned home to marry and take over the family business."

Smile bittersweet, Nerek replied, "I wish I could have met them too. Sadly, I would prefer you never meet my mother. She doesn't care for me, and she'd be unimpressed I settled for a mage-in-residence rather than someone useful, like a battle mage or a master healer. She's impossible to please. I gave up trying years ago."

"Well, you won't ever have to give up on me," Kohar replied, then grinned. "Especially with a cock—"

Nerek shoved him off the bed.

# THE CASTELLAN

Bedros was doing his level best to stay awake, but with the droning rain, his lap blanket toasty warm, his coffee and brandy even warmer, and the only thing to do reading reports on that season's crop yields from his tenants, staying awake was something even the gods would struggle to do.

Unfortunately, his only other choices were to read tax reports instead or go outside to see what all the earlier ruckus had been about. Though if Kohar or Nerek hadn't come to see him about it, the matter couldn't be too serious.

He managed to slog through another report, this one on the thrilling life of oats. Yields had exceeded expectations, which was good, because as usual, the winter was likely to be brutal and last seemingly forever.

Giving up, he scribbled a few last notes to himself and threw the papers aside, rising from his cozy cocoon of blankets and brandy to see what his castle residents were up to.

He hadn't taken a dozen steps when he crossed paths with one of the maids who maintained the rooms on that hall, including his own. "What was all that noise in the yard?"

"Some of the children got their hands on a few potions and thought it would be funny to give it to the chickens." The maid rolled her eyes. "Master Kohar was not amused, though he says the effects are harmless."

"Where did they get the potions?"

"From a traveling merchant stupid enough to leave his bags where curious children can inspect them," she replied with a sigh. "Kohar had some words for him; that was probably most of the shouting you heard. But all the chickens are bright colors now, and they've gotten loose everywhere. Kohar insisted the merchant be the one to gather them back up, and it's going…" She shrugged a shoulder and pressed her lips together in an attempt to stifle giggles before finally managing to finish, "Interestingly."

"Just another day at Castle Rehm," Bedros said with a laugh. "Thank you."

She curtsied and carried on, and Bedros headed for the great hall, where he was met with an irate Kohar, a frazzled stranger, and about a dozen or so chickens ranging in color from bright blue to dark purple, with a couple of orange and yellow for variety.

He nudged a plump turquoise rooster out of his way and went to join the harried-looking crowd at the table. "I've been hearing interesting tales, and I see they do not exaggerate. What manner of potion or potions could do this?"

It was Kohar's brother Taniel who replied, from where he was traipsing about the hall collecting fallen feathers in a small basket. "Festival potions. They're not really more than toys, which is probably why the children latched onto them. People use them to dye their hair for a few hours or to alter a dress for a day, that sort of thing. Easily made, easily used, easily foisted upon unsuspecting chickens."

"Also easily capable of killing children should they drink it like they're taught with healing draughts and the like," Kohar said from where he glowered at the merchant in a way that said murder was not yet dismissed as a possibility.

"I didn't anticipate they would paw through my belongings and steal them," the merchant replied.

That did nothing to soothe Kohar's ire. "You're not a very good merchant if you fail to anticipate something as basic and common as theft and stupid children."

"I'm to blame for being stolen from?"

"You're to blame for being stupid enough to leave untended toys where children were sure to find them."

"Enough," Bedros said. "Good sir, have you been reimbursed for your lost wares?"

The merchant tore his gaze from Kohar. "Yes, Your Grace. Master Kohar here saw to the matter. I apologize for the upheaval I've unintentionally caused."

Bedros waved the words aside. "I wish all our problems were as mild as rainbow chickens. Why are you collecting the feathers, Taniel?"

"Experiments, and possibly to mess with Kohar at a later date."

Bedros laughed. Kohar glared.

"I'm surprised Nerek isn't about."

"He's down at the armory having a word with some soldiers who decided to show up for duty still drunk."

"I see," Bedros said with a wince. Not so much for the soldiers, who were getting what they deserved, but for the rest of them while Nerek was in a bad mood. "Soothe the beast for us, would you?"

Kohar laughed. "Sit and have a late lunch with us, Your Grace."

Rolling his eyes at the formal address, because they were all well past such things in their Castle of the Middle of Nowhere, Bedros took a seat as Kohar sent one of the hall attendants to fetch him a bowl of what looked like a promising pixie soup. "So what else is going on today, other than crop yield reports, tax reports, and rainbow chickens? Will it affect the color of the meat?"

"No, it's entirely superficial. By the end of the day most of them will be back to normal, and any stragglers will definitely be white and brown again by morning."

"Pity, there's probably money to be made in such a peculiar thing." He scooped up a bite of potato and carrot. "Any other excitement I should be concerned about?"

"Maybe," Nerek said as he came striding in, rain sloughing from his light armor, making a mess the servants would kill him for when they caught him. "I've just gotten word from scouts at the eastern garrison that some nobleman and his retinue passed through headed this way. Asked specifically about you."

Bedros sighed and dropped his spoon in his bowl, abruptly no longer hungry. "Marvelous. I wonder who has come to bully me into doing His Majesty's bidding now. Did they glean any information?"

"Said it was a handsome fellow, dark skin and red-brown hair, brown eyes. Horses and armed escort wore a crest of a swallow—"

"Holding an arrow with dragon blood on the tip," Bedros finished. "That's impossible."

"I assure you it's not. Who is he?"

"Remember I told you I saved an old nemesis from taking the fall for one of the king's cronies?" When they nodded, he added, "Well, that nemesis I saved is apparently on his way to see me. Lord Warren Tellark, fifth Earl of Swallow's Nest." Bedros tapped his thumb against his mouth. "Why in the world would he be coming here?"

"Whatever the reason, you probably shouldn't

find out still wearing your lounging clothes," Kohar said.

Bedros sighed and looked down at himself. "I suppose you have a point. I'll be back momentarily."

Returning to his chambers, he called for hot water and a wash bin. When they arrived, along with his attendant, Macy, Bedros set to work making himself look like the duke he was mean to be, rather than the lord of a largely-forgotten castle that was his day-to-day.

At least the rain seemed to have stopped for now.

Why was Tellark coming to see him? They'd been all but mortal enemies since their school days. Well, no. The more time passed, the more Bedros was forced to look back and acknowledge that most of his problems, his 'enemies,' had been Rocco's enemies. There were a lot of things about Rocco he'd been forced to finally see ever since he'd taken the throne and stopped pretending to be anything but the bastard he was.

Had any part of the man he'd called friend since childhood been real? Or was Bedros simply the person he'd manipulated the most and best? Bedros wasn't really certain he wanted to know the answer.

"Thank you," he said as Macy stepped back to give him a final critical onceover. "I daresay I actually look like a prim and proper duke for once."

Macy laughed. "You always look like a duke, Your Grace. Now you look a bit more like a spoiled noble, without going entirely peacock."

"I appreciate it." He let Macy get on with the rest of his day, and headed back to the great hall, where Kohar and Nerek wasted no time in laughing at him.

"Go get dressed yourselves, you smart asses," he said, kicking Nerek's ankle idly—not that he'd have felt a real kick through his heavy boots. "I can't have my Captain of the Guard and Mages-in-Residence looking like hooligans. If I must look fancy, all of us must look fancy."

"What's the point?" Nerek groused. "Someone will come to me with a crisis before I'm finished dressing, and my good clothes will be ruined anyway."

Kohar tugged him to his feet. "Come along, Captain Scruffy. I'll make it worth your while."

"Quit that," Nerek said, and it was always endearing how pleased and flustered he looked at Kohar's flirtations. Bedros hadn't ever thought he'd see his strict, stony captain of the guard soften, but from the moment Kohar had arrived, Nerek had possessed all the fortitude of sun-warmed butter.

As the three departed, Taniel trailing behind the other two, Bedros sat and called for more soup and bread. It would probably be some time yet before Tellark arrived, and Bedros wanted to be as prepared as possible.

Try as he might, he still could not come up with any reason Tellark would be visiting him. Not least of all because Tellark's holding were clear on the opposite end of the continent. If Bedros seldom saw anything but snow, Tellark never saw anything but blistering sunshine. Bedros honestly wasn't certain which extreme was worse, though he definitely preferred the snow himself.

When the food came, it was accompanied by hot, spiced wine. Thanking the servant, he bent to making quick work of the meal, half-listening to the conversations buzzing around him. Rehm might be buried in snow most of the year, and the rest of it split pretty evenly between rain and sunshine, but they worked hard to make the best of what they had.

The tenants had been leery when he'd first

arrived, yet another twit noble who knew nothing of farming, let alone the peculiarities of Rehm, but Bedros wasn't completely spoiled. His family hadn't had any titles at all until he was twelve, and his father had only been a baron.

Finding himself packed off to a fancy school had changed everything for Bedros, and his world had shifted again when he'd somehow become friends with a royal prince. Though more and more, it seemed that he'd just been an easily manipulated fool, too naïve and stupid to realize why that prince hadn't already had piles of friends amongst his actual peers.

Bedros drew a deep breath and let it out slowly. It didn't matter. He'd seen sense eventually. Better late than never and all that. Rocco no longer had any control over him. Well, he did, but only that of a king over one of his subjects. What would Bedros's parents think, if they were still alive, to see their son had become a duke, but only because it was a handy, humiliating way to exile him to the ends of the earth?

Finished with his meal, Bedros placed the dishes on the table where they'd all be collected by the kitchen staff. When he'd first arrived, the great hall had been an ode to pretension—thrones, dais, expensive, difficult to maintain rugs and runners, the whole set. Hardly useful in a functional castle.

Now it was tables that were actually practical, rushes that were changed out every couple of days, and at night bedding was laid out for the majority of the staff to sleep. Past that, he'd largely let the castle residents make changes as they pleased, saving it from the rampant stupidity of the previous duke. Unsurprisingly, the fool had died because he'd decided to get appallingly drunk, and then in a drunken stupor had decided to go for a ride, and shortly after had frozen to death—and been completely naked when they'd found him, or so the story went. Apparently that was common in people who froze to death.

The horse had survived, though, and Bedros was quite fond of her.

Leaving the great hall, he headed down the short hallway that led to the enormous kitchen, which was at least half the size of the hall—the fireplace alone could fit several people, though as usual it was only filled with roasting meat and racks of bread. Some of it was for the castle, but a good portion of it was marked as belonging to various families in the village, who dropped stuff off for baking in the morning and picked it up a little before sunset.

His head cook and master of the kitchen, Liset, looked up from where she was deftly butchering a lamb. "Castle rumor is that you've just made my day infinitely more difficult, Your Grace."

Bedros smiled and paused to snitch a berry tart from a tray before joining her at the table and replied, "I'm afraid that's true, though in my defense, I didn't know we were going to have a visitor. That never happens around here."

"I hope this one brings less trouble than the last," Liset replied tartly.

"You and me both." Bedros bit into the tart, not quite groaning at how good it was. They were even better with fresh berries, but those were hard to come by in Rehm. Most often they traded for preserves and dried fruits with villages a bit further south who struggled less with the snow. "Anything you need me to commandeer for you?"

She smiled faintly. "We should be alright. I've got the lamb here, though it was meant for the Tidings of Winter meal. A pig roasting, and a few chickens. Should be plenty enough for a couple days' worth of proper meals."

"Your meals are always proper, and if His Lordship complains, he'll find himself eating snow, I assure you."

That got him a bigger smile, hard to earn from the stern Liset. Bedros returned it, and with a second snitched pie, hustled out of her kitchen before he got told to, because if it reached that point then suffering was guaranteed.

When he returned to the great hall, Nerek, Kohar, and Taniel had returned, his imposing Captain and two intimidating Mages-in-Residence. Normally such a small castle wouldn't require two mages, but after so many of his people had been killed by a succubus, Bedros wanted all the help he could get in making certain such a thing never happened again.

"I suppose now that we're all looking civilized, and the cook has dinner well in hand, we're as ready as we can be."

Kohar gave him a look. "Tell us why you and this earl are enemies."

"Back in our school days, it simply started out as a rivalry. I think one stupid thing after another turned the relationship hostile. After school, I was Rocco's obedient, loyal idiot, and Tellark, frankly, showed far more sense. It is shameful to admit, but the more I look back on it, the more painfully obvious it becomes that Rocco used me every step of the way.

"It wasn't until he took the throne that I started to see him as he really was, and by then... well, too little, too late." He rubbed the back of his neck, then let his hand fall with a sigh. "Tellark and I don't always agree on how to resolve problems, or on certain policies that come up in the Hall, but mostly I hated him because Rocco told me that we should. To be honest, exiling me here was probably the best thing he did for all of us, though I'm in no hurry to do *him* any favors."

"I know the type," Nerek said quietly. "I grew up with her. The only reason I figured my mother out as quickly as I did was because she was fond of beating me when I really pissed her off, and the more time passed, the quicker she was to anger. You're not to blame, and better to figure it out late than to never figure it out at all. I'm glad you escaped that life."

"Me too. Thank you."

Kohar smiled briefly. "Here I thought I had it rough because I had to figure out how to prostitute myself for spending money without my aunt or parents finding out."

Bedros laughed as Taniel and Nerek rolled their eyes.

"Stop making it sound like Mother and Father never gave us an allowance. You just always spent yours all on the first day."

"I did not."

"I am not going to play this game with you."

"Good. Be a proper younger brother and shut up."

Taniel stuck his tongue out, and Kohar made a face at him, and Nerek heaved the sigh of the eternally suffering. He turned to Bedros. "Do I need to be prepared to throw him out?"

"I doubt it. That's not really his style. If it were, he and Rocco probably would have been friends instead of enemies." Bedros rubbed the back of his neck as his thoughts tumbled and turned. "You might want to be ready for whoever comes soon after him, though. It wouldn't surprise me at all if he was trying to beat someone here. There's no other reason he'd come. Any other scenario, I'd be receiving messages. No, somebody wants to show up as a nasty little surprise and catch me unprepared. Tellark is ahead of them. Why, I cannot begin to guess, but warning me—or whatever he's doing—must be the lesser evil."

"You did save his life," Kohar replied. "He could be repaying a debt."

"Always a possibility, I suppose." Though Bedros doubted it. After years upon years of him and Rocco making Tellark's life difficult, Bedros had piles upon piles of debt still to repay. Tellark owed him nothing, and they both knew it.

Which just made this visit even more alarming. Something must be truly horrible if Tellark was trying to reach him about it before whoever Rocco had sent. If it were just a simple assassination or some such he wouldn't bother.

Horns sounded, announcing someone was approaching. "Guess we're about to find out," Bedros said.

Nerek departed, guards falling into place around and behind him as he beckoned. Bedros followed more leisurely, flanked by his mages. He waited on the steps, Nerek and his soldiers spreading out around the courtyard in a minimal protective circle.

In the distance, he could see the carriage, with a well-armed escort, racing toward him. It really was Tellark.

The carriage approached quickly and yet seemed to take years, and Bedros was ready to scream by the time the portcullis was raised and the carriage came thundering down the road and through the entryway into the ward.

It came to an abrupt stop, and stable hands rushed in to start tending the exhausted horses. Guards dismounted, and one swung open the door of the carriage.

Seeing Tellark again was like a kick to the nuts. The last time they'd seen each other had been the morning after Tellark had been released from prison and Bedros was packing all that he could manage in the two hours Rocco had given him to get the hells out of the city.

Tellark had been bruised, battered, and gaunt from his brutal months-long stay in prison, while Rocco and his cronies worked diligently to ensure they could execute him without suffering consequences, and that his death would take at least a few problems with him. Waste not, want not, and all that.

He'd been angry, exhausted, and resentfully grateful for Bedros's help, which Bedros had honestly thought was more than fair. Bedros had dismissed the words and handed off a note before departing, bound for the ends of the earth, where he'd honestly expected to die within weeks, at best months, of some unfortunate accident.

Instead Rocco had tried to force him into marriage, and then it seemed had opted to go back to ignoring him.

"Tellark," Bedros greeted. "Not a visitor I ever thought to have here at Castle Rehm, but uh, be welcome."

"Akari." Tellark looked him up and down, expression pensive, pretty brown eyes as sharp and observant as ever. Whatever he saw, the way his face shuttered said he found Bedros wanting, but that was neither unexpected nor unfair. "I see you're doing well."

"Certainly can't complain. Come inside before it starts raining again."

Tellark headed for him, then stopped short. "Why in the world is that chicken lilac?" His confusion grew as the lilac chicken was promptly followed by a green, yellow, and sky blue one. "Never mind." He climbed the steps and bowed stiffly. "I apologize for arriving with neither invitation nor notice."

"I think, given the long list of crimes to my name, I can permit a token bit of rudeness," Bedros replied, and clapped him on the back. "Come on. Let's get you something to drink to clear the dust from the road, and you can tell me why you're here. I'm assuming His High and Mightiness is up to something?"

Looking bemused, Tellark followed him into the keep and to the end of the middle row of tables, close to the fire, where servants had already arranged wine, beer, and food aplenty. Tellark's frown deepened, but he said nothing, only took the seat Bedros indicated and after prompting, said he'd prefer wine.

Once drinks were poured and a plate had been filled for Tellark, Bedros rested his folded arms on the table, leaning in slightly. "So what direst circumstances brought you all the way up here to see me, instead of sending an emissary or a messenger?"

"War," Tellark said flatly. "My own people have scattered across the country, some even leaving the country, so nothing that happens to me for my defiance will come down on them. I'm sure it's only a matter of time before His Majesty strips me of everything, if he hasn't already. It was worth all that, though, because he needs a war with Serren. What could be a better reason to start that war than avenging the death of the Duke of Rehm, his beloved friend, heartlessly slaughtered by invading forces, along with every other person in the castle and nearby village."

Bedros sighed. "I should have guessed he'd take that path eventually. By why? Tormay has never had any quarrel with Serren, and the forces garrisoned just across the border definitely have no quarrel with Rehm." On the contrary, they and the village they 'protected' traipsed about all the time. There was a long-standing tradition of 'booze, sex, peace, and tranquility' between Rehm and the Serrens across the border in Valta Village and the Valta Garrison. The last major quarrel had involved some stolen horses that had proven to be just a huge, bizarre comedy of errors. Nearly everyone spoke some measure of both languages, and if anyone ever bothered to sit down and sort out the precise parentage of many of the children, there'd be drama enough to last for years.

"The short answer is greed," Tellark said. "I can give you the long one if you like."

"We'll save it for a night when I'm so desperately bored I want to catch up on politics," Bedros said. "When are my people and I to be heartlessly murdered?"

"Unless plans have changed, the attack is to happen in three to five days. He's sending Vare to speak with you first, but he's also getting forces into position so they're ready to move quickly in the aftermath."

Next to Bedros, Nerek looked angrier than Bedros had ever seen him, and that included the recent mess with the succubus, which had involved Nerek's cousin. "Let me guess: General Kara is in charge of this one."

Surprise filled Tellark's face briefly. "How did you know that?"

"I know my mother. There's nothing she loves more than needless slaughter dressed up as heroics," Nerek replied. "Excuse me." He surged to his feet and stormed off, probably to begin preparations. He'd come find Bedros later if there were supplies and equipment he needed signed off on.

"His mother. Poor bastard." Tellark shook his head and refilled his cup. "Normally I'd be more than happy to let you rot, Akari, but I won't let thousands of innocents die, or the hundreds of thousands that will follow after this little drama concludes. So here I am."

"Here you are," Bedros echoed. "I assume you'll be remaining with us indefinitely, since going anywhere else is guaranteed suicide?"

Tellark grimaced, which was reply enough, and drank more wine.

Well, it wasn't like Bedros had ever thought Tellark would be delighted by spending extended lengths of time in his company. He didn't think he deserved to be thought of as a fate worse than death, but then again, Tellark had all the reason in the world to hate him, no point in being childish and defensive about it now.

Shunting aside thoughts of his fragile ego, Bedros put his mind back on vastly more important matters. "Kohar, Taniel, what sort of defenses can you muster in so short a time?"

"Plenty," Taniel said, looking like a cat about to harass some rainbow-colored chickens. "They'll be expensive."

Bedros waved the words aside. "I don't care about money. I care about lives. Get to work. I'm sure Nerek is already arranging to get information from across the border, one of you might want to tag along, or at least send his chosen scout with a list of questions and supplies of your own. Get someone down to the village to speak with Chief Dalin so she can start getting people moved here to the castle and closing up the village and get word to people farther afield."

His people scattered, including the maid who'd been standing around listening, who immediately vanished off to the kitchens at a nod from Bedros. "Come on, I'm sure you'd like some rest now that you've delivered your news. I—" he stopped as thunder abruptly crashed, drowning out the rest of the world and shaking the whole castle. It was followed by lightning and a rush of rain that promised the next few days would be absolutely miserable, especially for the poor staff forced to keep on top of the inevitable mess. "Definitely nothing better to do now, and it's only going to get colder."

Tellark looked at him oddly. "Colder? But it's only September."

Bedros laughed, though not without sympathy. Rehm and its weather took a bit of adjusting. "You're in the mountains now, Tellark. You're lucky there's no snow yet. We'll just barely finish with the year's harvest before we're buried. I wouldn't be surprised if some of this turns to ice overnight. Don't worry, though; I'd never let a guest of mine freeze to death. We'll see you're fixed right up with warm clothes and everything else you'll need."

He got Tellark to his feet, let the poor bastard take some wine with him for consolation, and escorted him up the stairs and through the halls to one of the rooms that wasn't far down from his. He pointed a thumb at the double doors to his room. "Those are my chambers, should you need anything, day or night. If I'm not there, I'm nearly always in the hall or the ward, and if by some chance I'm pulled away from those three places, it probably won't be hard to find me, as that normally only happens when there's a crisis. Otherwise, I stay where I'm out of the way and easily found. Your room should be ready, and if you lack for anything, simply speak with one of the guards stationed here. They'll be happy to see you get it. I assume you have further belongings coming?"

"A cart. It should arrive in the next few days, along with a couple of my servants."

"We'll be ready. Rest well." Bedros strode off to his own chambers, ignoring the bewildered, frustrated look that had filled Tellark's face.

Alone again, and superfluous for the present as

his people made ready to avoid being the sacrificial lamb for their king's war, Bedros reluctantly went back to reading crop yields and tax reports.

He'd just finished the last of the crop reports when a frantic knocking came at his door. "Come in!"

His chatelaine, Mariana, strode into the room. "Your Grace, pardon to disturb, but we've a bit of a problem in the ward."

"What's wrong?"

"It's flooded, and none of us noticed until it got high enough to start spilling into the hall."

"Well, that's a new one. I'll be right down. Make certain the children don't go anywhere near it. I wouldn't put it past a few of them to try swimming, and gods alone knows what's in that water if something has backed it up. Nobody else is to go out and try to fix the problem. I'll handle it."

"Yes, Your Grace."

She left, and Bedros discarded his fine clothes for an older, far more worn set, not bothering with more than a shirt since all the fabric would just make it harder to move once it got soaked. Then he pulled on thigh-high boots and laced them snuggly and secured his hair tightly, so it would hopefully stay out of his way. Last he pulled on a hooded cowl, leather and water-proofed, to further keep his hair from collapsing around him and hopefully let him see a little better.

Downstairs, staff were working frantically to keep the great hall from becoming a pond. Opening the doors would be a fool's game, so in lieu of that Bedros scaled the wall to one of the windows, cast aside the heavy tapestry covering it, and climbed onto the wide sill.

Below, his ward *had* become a pond. Thankfully, it didn't look as though people or animals had drowned in it. Well, the likeliest explanation was that the rain had swept something into the drain that was supposed to keep this from happening.

"What in the world are you doing up there?"

Bedros turned slightly and stared down at Tellark. "The ward is flooding. I'm going to go figure out what's causing it. Hopefully the matter will be easily resolved. Back in a bit!" He pulled up his hood and then swung out and down, clinging tightly and moving slowly, until he was far enough down he could jump the rest of the way with relative safety.

The clogged drain and the storm had worked with brutal efficiency; the water was already up to his thighs and still rising. That certainly spoke to the skills of the original architects, though maybe they could have added a secondary drain. He'd add to the list of projects for spring and summer.

He waded across the ward, shoving aside escaped barrels and runaway root vegetables, pulled away from his mission briefly by the most wretched looking cat he'd ever seen, hunched on a floating crate and mewling piteously.

After he'd gotten the poor thing shoved into the stable via a window, he returned to the primary quest. The drain for the ward was in a portion of the curtain behind the stables, a circle that was half in the ground, half in the curtain, and protected by crossed iron bars. Every now and then something got in them and caused a slight backup—usually a dead bird left by the cats or something blown in by the wind, left by melting snow. Rarely was it something that blocked the entire drain, which was what must have happened this time for the ward to fill so quickly.

It was impossible to see anything above the water; it was too murky, and the rain was coming down too hard anyway. Under the water wouldn't be much better, so he'd have to hope that touch alone would let him deduce—and solve—the problem.

Taking a deep breath, Bedros plunged beneath the icy water and made quickly for the location of the drain. As feared, he couldn't see much, only murky shadows and churning bits of debris.

The real problem was that he couldn't find the drain. He found the curtain, where the stones that lined the opening stuck out a bit, but beyond that, all he felt was rock. Piles and piles…

Someone had blocked it on purpose. Why? That was for later. Bedros grabbed and started throwing. He had to surface for air, but then was right back down, hauling away all that he could, shoving and pushing and kicking rocks aside as he best he could until he saw at least some of the grating.

Thankfully, the water began to move after that. Only slightly, but any movement at all was better than none. Bedros took a moment to rest, his chest heaving from exertion, so cold he could barely feel his fingers anymore.

When he was as recovered as he was going to get, he set back to work, focusing on the larger, heavier stones. They took some work and a few trips for air each, but at last he got them moved well enough out of the way that the water could begin to drain in earnest.

After that, he simply stood by to keep the rocks from being pushed right back into the grating and waited as the water steadily lowered.

Several minutes and forever later, the ward was mostly clear, though it wouldn't be one hundred percent until the rain stopped. Slogging back to the keep, shivering the whole way, Bedros pounded on the doors.

One of them almost immediately swung open, and Mariana cried out in relief and yanked him inside, hugging him tightly. "You're all right, Your Grace!"

"Takes more than a thorough soaking to do me

in, I assure you." He hugged her back, then withdrew so he didn't get her clothes any wetter. "I don't suppose I could have some warm clothes brought to me?"

She sniffed in offense. "Waiting by the fire, of course, and a proper toddy too."

"You're finer than any queen, Mariana."

She sniffed again, but bustled off with a pleased smile, calling out to various maids and footmen so they could get to work cleaning the water and mud up once and for all.

Someone brought a bench over, and Bedros sat to begin the laborious process of removing laced up thigh-high boots that were covered in water and muck. Thankfully, a couple of footmen were willing to help, and he had them off in several minutes instead of several hours. He made quick work of his clothes, and wrapped up in the drying robe a maid offered before finally heading over to the fire to put on proper clothes.

They were toasty warm as he pulled them on, even the soft, fur-lined boots he pulled on. He groaned as he sat at one of the benches and dragged his hot toddy close. "I am never doing that again. Would somebody see if it's possible for Nerek and Kohar to come see me? If not, I'll speak with them when it is possible."

"Think they're trapped in the armory at present," said one of the maids. "I tried to get out there to deliver some food earlier, and everything was just mud and water."

"I see." Bedros sighed. "We'll face that problem when the rain stops, then. Hopefully they have supplies enough in there." Though the armory was Nerek's domain, and he was nothing if not prepared for every contingency. He took another sip of his toddy, which was marvelous.

Unfortunately, from the small horde of staff

waiting at the fringes, he wasn't going to be allowed to savor it. He waved them closer. "Who's next?"

Liset approached, hands wrapped fretfully in her apron. "I'm sorry, Your Grace, but these rains… I don't know what's happening, but the south ward is flooding something awful, too. I've already set people upon it, since it's not flooded as bad as the front was before we caught it, but between that and all the water coming in the kitchen and putting my fires out, I'm not going to be able to have a proper dinner for you and your guest."

"I think if that is the biggest complaint we have tonight, we all have the sense to count ourselves fortunate. Whatever you can put together, my dear, we will eat gladly. We're all adults here. We can deal with a few cold plates, or no food at all if we must. As long as the children, elderly, and sick are taken care of."

"Your Grace." Liset bobbed a quick curtsey and they bustled off, two of the others in the group falling in behind her—clearly they'd come as back up or witnesses, or something along those lines.

"Next," Bedros said with a smile.

Two stable hands approached. "Your Grace, we've been into the stables to look them over once the flooding was cleared. We're still doing a more thorough inspection…"

"But clearly there was some serious damage discovered?"

They nodded in unison, and the shorter of the two said, "Two of the horses took significant injury. Looks like they panicked in their stalls, and just weren't enough of us in there at the time to calm all of them. Ain't none severe enough to be put down, thankfully, but they'll have to be sedated by the mages and taken to the village for proper fixing up."

"Of course. I believe our resident mages are

currently trapped in the armory, but I'll compose a list of what we need from them and add your request. Are the horses well enough for now?"

"Yessir—I mean, yes, Your Grace."

Bedros waved off the mistake. "Very well. Let me know if that changes." The stable hands departed, and the next pair, some maids, approached with more water-related issues.

Three hours and two toddies later, Bedros was ready for a nap. On the positive side, he seemed to have addressed all current problems that he could. He added his cup to the table where dishes were put for staff to collect later and yawned as he weighed his options for what little daylight remained. "I suppose I should make my way to the armory, though I'm not looking forward to all that mud and water again."

"I can do it, if you want."

Bedros turned, startled, and stared at Tellark, who was sitting at one of the other tables, sipping what looked like a mug of tea. "How long have you been there?"

"The whole time," Tellark replied, and smiled ever so fleetingly, like he wasn't certain he should be doing it. "You're not what I expected, Akari."

"Bedros is fine. Even the staff doesn't stand much on formality when they aren't putting their best manners forward in front of guests. We're busy enough around this place without all the bother of tiresome formalities that just slow everything down."

"Bedros, then," Tellark replied. "Did you want me to get to the armory?"

"I'm not going to have you risking your neck making that trek. That's no way to treat a guest, especially one who has come all this way with information that has very likely saved lives."

Tellark laughed. "I'm not so frail a guest I can't

do here what I more or less do at home. You might deal with more cold and snow, but I promise I deal with more rain and mud, and sand is even worse. Let me get the proper gear for it. If there are messages or anything you'd like me to deliver, write them now." He vanished without waiting for a reply.

Bedros thought about going after him, or resuming the discussion when he returned, but the truth of the matter was that he was exhausted. Swimming, diving, hauling heavy rocks under water—such work drained a person quickly, no matter how fit they were. He wasn't honestly certain he could do practically the same again, and in the increasing dark.

So he surrendered and called for pen and paper, and a waterproof case to transport his letters. Thankfully, writing everything up for Nerek, Kohar, and Taniel was an easy enough matter. By the time he finished, Tellark had returned.

Gods preserve his sanity, did the man have to look so ridiculously distracting in thigh high boots? In clothes that were entirely too form fitting? The world must really hate him, that he kept noticing that Tellark was ridiculously attractive. There were clearly a lot of things that Tellark was willing to do to save lives, but Bedros would be willing to bet kissing him wasn't one of them.

Well, he supposed he was getting what he deserved, after a fashion.

"Are those your letters?"

"Yes. Thank you for helping. I hope you do not come to any harm."

"If I can survive swimming with sharks, I can probably survive a bit of mud." Tellark smiled briefly, tucked the notes away, and then Bedros showed him to the steps that led from the castle down to the armory. The problem with living on a hill was that steps were required for everything, and steps were a shockingly easy way for people to die.

The rain was still coming down relentlessly, getting colder by the minute. It very likely would turn to sleet before the night was out, which would just compound all their problems. Delightful.

Down at the bottom of the steps was a veritable lake of mud and water. There was so much of it, they probably could not physically get the doors open, and even if they could, they'd only succeed in flooding the armory.

"This shouldn't have happened," Bedros said, and when Tellark gave him a questioning look added, "The flooding. This mud. I do actually ensure the castle is well-maintained. It has to be, or we'd never survive the snow that buries us at least half the year. Someone purposefully blocked the drain in the ward, and I suspect something equally nefarious happened here."

"Someone trusted to the rain when they set up your castle to fail? That is quite the gamble."

"Not really. The rain, the snow… it all runs like expensive clockwork. The oldest villagers can practically tell you to the day and the hour when the rain and snow will start. Anybody who listened for ten minutes would have a pretty good idea of when to act."

"I see." Tellark pulled up the hood of his cloak, which looked to be specially treated to repel water. "I'll be back as soon as I can."

"I'll leave guards here to escort you back, or get me should something go wrong. Be careful. If it seems safer to give up, then do so."

Tellark gave a playful salute and vanished into the deluge. Bedros watched him for several minutes, then had to turn away before he gave himself a heart attack from the stress and worry.

Instead, he had lamps brought, along with his

paperwork from upstairs, and interspersed tackling his unending correspondence with helping with problems that came along around the castle. The biggest concern was getting it ready for an influx of guests. That would keep the majority of his staff busy the rest of the night and all of tomorrow, and things would only get crazier as people started to arrive. Hopefully the rain would stop long enough to make it a bit more manageable, but Bedros wasn't holding his breath.

He ceased with his paperwork when dinner started coming out of the kitchens, sending a footman off with it to return to his chambers. Instead of eating, however, he went back off down the hall to the stairs that led to the armory. "Any sign of Lord Tellark?"

"No, sir," one of the guards said. "But I'm thinking with the dark and rain, he opted to stay put until morning. Be the smart thing, eh?"

"Just so. Very well. If I'm still asleep when he does return, see I am woken at once."

"Yes, sir."

He gripped their shoulders in thanks, then returned to the hall and took his seat, eating at a leisurely pace, letting his mind turn as he half-listened to the music that started up at one point, one of the stable hands with his lute and an upstairs maid on her pipes.

It could almost have been any other night in the castle, save there wasn't nearly as much laughter. Everyone was too tired or too worried. Even the music didn't last as long as usual, and soon they were all cleaning up and shuffling away. Bedros returned to his own chambers and prepared for bed. Normally he'd be up for a few more hours, but he wanted to be up bright and early to better organize and tackle the long day ahead.

*~*~*

It was still dark when Macy shook him awake. "Must I?" he groaned.

"You insisted it happen."

"I hate me," Bedros said with another groan, but sat up and threw back the blankets. That immediately resulted in swearing, and him hating absolutely everything in life. "I see it's going to be a nice, pleasant morning."

Laughing, Macy helped him get into warm clothes suitable for trekking in and out of the castle all day and a new pair of thigh-high boots since his other ones were still drying out. When his hair had been braided and pinned, Macy then helped him into a waist-length jacket made of fine wool and trimmed in fur. Hopefully the day would warm up, but if not, he was prepared. "Thank you, Macy."

He left Macy to tidy the room and headed off downstairs, where he was greeted by the sight of Nerek, Kohar, and the others sitting around eating breakfast. "I told them to wake me when you were first seen returning."

"We went to wake you, sir—that is, Your Grace," one of the nearby guards said, "but Mistress Mariana said that Macy had already gone to wake you for the day so not to worry."

"Ah. Thank you." Bedros took his usual seat at the table near the fire and thanked the maid who brought him a plate of food and a large, steaming cup of tea. "So how was your night in the armory?"

"Noisy," Nerek said.

"Boring," Kohar added. "I wasn't allowed to have any fun."

Nerek glared at him, cheeks going red. "Shut up."

Taniel rolled his eyes. "I had to listen to that all night. Your letter certainly had me thinking, though. The sort of sabotage you spoke of would have to be done quickly, efficiently. People who knew what they were doing and could go unnoticed, more than a little tricky around here, where everybody knows one another."

"So they likely worked at night and counted on the weather to ensure nobody noticed the problem. That doesn't explain the ward," Bedros said. "It was fine before Tellark arrived. Why wait until later in the day to do that?"

"Maybe it failed the first time, and they had to redo it," Nerek said.

Bedros nodded and gulped tea before working on his porridge, which was laden with nuts, honey, and dried berries. "Whatever the case, it is clear that our friends in the royal castle are trying to help the matter of our defeat along. Makes me wonder why Rocco is bothering to send Vare at all."

"Who is Vare?" Taniel asked.

"The Royal Castellan," Nerek, Tellark, and Bedros replied. Tellark continued, "He's become Rocco's favorite lackey, after Bedros decided enough was enough." His face pinched in a look that Bedros couldn't interpret. "Though the impression in the capital is that you are less in exile and more doing His Majesty's bidding on an undisclosed matter. Many believe you're still his lackey, at least to some degree."

Bedros grimaced and stabbed at his porridge with his spoon. "I spent the majority of my life thinking we were friends. Looking back, it's pathetically obvious I was never any such thing." He sighed. "Just a lonely, out of place boy eager to fit in somewhere—anywhere. Easy pickings, as they say on the streets."

"It's little wonder he and my mother get along

so well," Nerek said sourly. "I fervently hope we resolve this mess before I have to deal with her."

"I didn't even know she had a son," Tellark said, "and I pride myself on my knowledge of the court and all its key players."

"My mother goes out of her way to ensure no one knows about her greatest and most lasting disappointment." Nerek finished his food and shoved it away. "To be honest, that has always suited me fine. I am off to the village to start moving people here. Hopefully the weather holds for most of the day."

"If it doesn't, keep people moving anyway, and we'll sort out the whole soggy mess when they get here," Bedros said. "Leave me a few guards, though, to run the perimeter with me. I want to see if I can find anymore sabotage."

"Can't you just stay here where it's safe?" Nerek asked.

"No."

Sighing, Nerek replied, "Fine," before striding off, guards milling nearby immediately falling into step around and behind him.

"I'll go with you," Taniel said. "I want to ensure our wards haven't been tampered with and modify them a bit."

"Is there something I can do?" Tellark asked. "I am here indefinitely, I may as well make myself useful."

"You can certainly supervise the preparing of the castle for me and oversee repairs and fortifications. Normally I'd leave the perimeter check to Nerek and remain here where I'm most useful, but…" Bedros spread his hands. "I need about six of me right now."

"I can manage a castle, especially as your staff needs little in the way of managing," Tellark said with a faint smile. "It shall be done."

Bedros stood. "Then I guess it's time to get to work. Kohar, good luck with whatever you'll be working on around here. Send an alert should you need me."

"Of course. Be careful out there, Bedros."

"I'll try."

He headed off, Taniel at his side, and as they reached the stables, several guards joined them, every last one decked out to go to war. "We're running perimeter, not hunting bandits."

"We do what the Captain says," replied Corsair, one of Nerek's lieutenants.

"Fair enough."

Bedros mounted up as a stable boy brought the horse he favored for such ventures, a handsome roan stallion he'd bought for cheap because it was too 'spirited' to be fit for a proper noble. Heaven forbid a horse not want to spend its life pulling carriages and escorting lazy bastards about town on a drunken spree.

As ever, the horse was more than adequately equipped with everything he could possibly need for the day ahead of them.

They rode off, the guards falling in around him and Taniel, heading west to start the perimeter check at that end and work their way all the way around, then loop back to the castle.

It didn't take long before they found signs of sabotage—abandoned sabotage, if he had to guess. "See if you can find them. This is recent."

Three of the guards rode off, and Bedros dismounted, patting his horse affectionately before going over to where at least three people had been cutting down an enormous old, dying tree. Once fallen, it would have gone a long way to blocking the stream that provided water for the castle and village, and he suspected a few more felled trees would have finished the job.

By the time anyone in the village or castle had noticed, the weather likely would have made it impossible to do anything about it. All the flooding and mud combined with an abrupt loss of water they could actually drink would have made for a particularly nasty disaster.

Whoever was pulling the strings on this desperately wanted them to stand no chance whatsoever in defending themselves when they were attacked. Strange way to go about winning a battle that only one side would know about until too bloody late, but effective for keeping it short, leaving no chance for anything that might turn the tide or otherwise upset the plan.

"That tree will have to come down; if left as is, rain and wind will finish the job. Stand watch while I take care of it."

He retrieved one of the abandoned axes and several of the felling wedges, and set to work chopping the tree down in a way that it would fall well clear of the stream.

It took him no small amount of time, as the job was arduous enough that three people really were required to do it efficiently. But he did finish it, sweaty and grimy and utterly exhausted at the end.

One of the guards brought him water and relieved him of the axe. "Impressive work, Your Grace."

"I assure you, my father would have found at least twenty things to criticize. He had me helping with the chopping since I was ten, and the felling since I was twelve. Getting a title didn't really mean much to him at the end of the day, when it came to work that needed to be done." He finished drinking and handed the half-empty skin back. "Thank you. Shall we press on? No word from the guards who gave chase?"

"No," Lieutenant Corsair said. "I'm not concerned yet, but I will be in another half hour."

"As you wish." They rode on, eyes sweeping carefully—Bedros and Taniel for signs of sabotage, the guards for signs of eminent violence.

Unfortunately, what they found was signs of recent violence, by way of the missing guards. Dead, and not neatly.

"They were stunned with magic first," Taniel said, dismounting and going to kneel by the nearest body. "Whoever did this, they have a mage of no small acumen amongst their numbers." His mouth flattened. "I have an educated guess on who that might be, given we're still trying to find him."

"Vosgi? You really think so? Surely they'd have brought their own. The capital is swimming in mages."

"Not like this," Taniel replied grimly. "These men were struck with a paralysis spell. Those are laborious work. To suitably paralyze something the size of a grown man would take at least four hours of work per spell, and there are three dead men here. That's a whole day's work used up in minutes. How many royal mages, even with lackies, do you know that could and would do such a thing?"

"None," Bedros conceded with a grimace. "They'd consider my 'backwater soldiers' a waste of such magic. How would they have known about him? Or found him, I guess, but why… never mind, the details little matter. What matters is Vosgi strikes again, and this time he's in league with far worse than a greedy mercenary." He motioned to Corsair. "Send someone back to inform Nerek of what's happened, and let's continue on. The perimeter check is more important than ever now."

"Yes, Your Grace." Corsair sent one of his men

off, leaving only him and two others total.

Pressing on, they swept along the path that wove through the mountain path that had served as an informal border between Tormay and Serren before politicians had gotten together and insisted on a fancy wall and gate a couple more miles north. Even now, it was still called the border path, and soon they'd be passing the field that had been used as a market and for other gatherings by the two countries for longer than the countries had existed. Politicians cared about borders, not people. The guards at the gate knew every face that traveled through, and the rare new guards swiftly learned them. The rest of the world might see two countries, two towns, and a looming wall between them, but everyone in the area saw a sprawling community with a stupid gate in the way.

"The weather is far too nice for all this cloak and dagger nonsense," Taniel said. "I'm sorry that yet again my poor past decisions are causing all of you problems."

"All of *us* problems, and it's not your fault Vosgi has an unhealthy fixation. No one is a greater victim at this point than you, unless you enjoy having an ex-lover stalk and harass you for daring to speak up about his illegal doings."

Taniel made a face. "I keep hoping one of his own spells will reduce him to ashes, or otherwise render him dead."

"Never give up hope," Bedros said. "In the meantime, we should probably hunt him more actively once this latest matter is concluded."

"I've been looking the whole damn time, but he's hiding from me, the stupid coward."

"Nerek's had us looking, too, as we're able, but no luck. This Vosgi is a wily bastard, and I fear what it will take to finally bring him in," Corsair said, "but one problem at a time, I suppose."

"Pending war does take precedence," Bedros replied. "Anything here, Tani?"

Taniel shook his head. "No. However Vosgi and the army found each other, they must be using him for people more than messing with our wards. Which is good, because even with me and my brother combined, that would be a nasty fight, and I can't honestly say we'd win."

"I really can't wait to kill this bastard once and for all," Bedros said. Killing was never his first choice, or even his tenth, but people like Vosgi wouldn't stop until someone else forced the matter.

Taniel said, "He better hope I don't get to him first."

They pressed on, riding and checking, even when the beautiful weather started to turn, and the temperature dropped enough that the returning rain would bring ice with it.

"Going to be a nasty winter," Corsair said with a sigh.

Bedros grunted in agreement as he pulled up his cowl to fend off the increasingly chilly wind. "Everybody warned me it would happen in the next couple of years. We're prepared. Food aplenty, work and amusement aplenty, and of course enough alcohol to sink several ships, because gods forbid this valley go one day without a drink."

Corsair laughed. Unlike most of the guards, who'd come with Nerek or shown up since, he was from the area, had left it only to complete his training and climb the ranks. Most of the money he made, he had sent directly to his family in the village, keeping only the smallest part of it for himself. "Come on, let's finish this and go warm up."

"I'm surprised Nerek hasn't found us to yell at

us yet," Taniel said. "Well, yell at Bedros."

"I was wondering about that myself, but Nerek is much busier than usual, so he's probably saving it all up," Bedros replied dryly.

At Corsair's urging, they resumed their ride, which thankfully only turned up one more point of sabotage—though that one point was bad enough. It was a bridge that spanned a gorge, at the bottom of which was a lot of nothing, the river that had cut it long dried up before anyone had turned the mountain valley into a home.

Unfortunately, repairing the damage that likely would have sent the next group of people or a heavy cart and its occupants to the bottom of the gorge would take more skill than they had readily to hand.

Bedros roped it off on either end, ignoring admonishments from Corsair, and affixed his seal, carved into fist-sized pieces of wood that he carried with him for precisely this sort of reason, to both ends. Once they were back at the castle, he'd see about securing the proper people to repair it.

They doubled back on the border path until it split, and took an alternate bridge further up the gorge. It meant getting home would take longer, but they'd be alive to do it.

Halfway there, however, a guard found them, red-faced and exhausted, his horse gleaming with sweat. "Your Grace!"

"What's wrong?"

"Lord Dier Vare has arrived, and demands your immediate presence. That's not the important part, though." His mouth settled in a grim line.

"Is anyone hurt?" Bedros asked. "Please don't tell me he's already started killing people."

"He was practically ready to execute Lord Tellark on the spot as a traitor to the crown. Master

Kohar prevented it, but…"

"But what, damn it?"

"Sorry, Your Grace. Lord Vare insisted that by being present at Castle Rehm, Lord Tellark was in violation of… frankly more than I could keep up with. The end result was that he was to be arrested and quite likely executed as this was a 'time of war,' more or less. Master Kohar halted the matter by claiming that you and Lord Tellark are married, a secret you did not intend on sharing until the new year, given the current political tension."

Bedros stared at him. Repeated the words over in his head, and then did it a third time. Finally he said, "I see."

"The whole castle is falling into the ruse, but it obviously won't hold with Your Grace being unaware of your marital status. Lord Vare was forbidding anyone leave the keep, but I managed to sneak out and borrow a horse from one of the soldiers returning from the village."

"He'll want proof," Bedros said. "I don't have marriage documents."

Taniel laughed. "I can manage that if you get me the time to do it. I can do marriage contracts in my sleep, I've written so many of the blasted things. Twenty minutes to write them up, ten minutes for the ink to sufficiently dry, and I'll ensure they don't look brand new too."

"I'm increasingly alarmed by the scope of your knowledge and skill," Bedros said. "So be it. Let's go greet my husband after a long day of running perimeter."

"Congratulations, Your Grace," Corsair said.

"Oh, be quiet." Bedros signaled his horse to move, and they rode off as quickly as they dared, especially as the sleet started to fall.

By the time they reached the castle, Bedros couldn't feel his fingers or his nose, and he was fairly certain he would not thaw until spring.

True to form, though, Vare loomed over him the moment he strode into the great hall. "It's about time—"

"I am soaked and half-frozen, Vare," Bedros snapped. "Let me have half a moment to make myself functional, even presentable, before you start in with whatever you've come to bully me about."

Fury immediately filled Vare's face, but Bedros walked on, headed for his chambers. "You'd better not have mistreated my people while I was out, or harangued my husband."

"Get back here at—"

Bedros reached the stairs that led up to his room and took them two at a time, even as his legs protested the abuse.

As he reached the door however, it was to see guards posted. "What's wrong that you're watching my door?"

"We're ensuring Lord Tellark is left in peace," one of them replied.

"Of course. Thank you." Bedros slipped inside, and was relieved to see that warm clothes, food, and a hot toddy were already waiting for him.

Also his husband, who naturally looked less than pleased by his abrupt change in status. Bedros closed the door and locked it. "I'll have a copy of the key made for you once everything has settled a bit. Until then, hold on to this one."

Tellark took the key without a comment, exhaustion and anger and fear cutting deep lines into his face. "I did not mean to bring this sort of upheaval."

"Believe me, no one thinks you showed up planning an elaborate scheme of pending war and royal plots to trick me into marriage, Tellark. I'm fairly certain you would, understandably, rather be married to a pumpkin."

That got him a laugh, weak but true. Tellark smiled faintly. "You're not a fate worse than death, Bedros. I admit we have history, but it's hard to overlook that you threw away literally your whole life to save mine. Seeing you here, at Castle Rehm… it's not been what I expected. I can count on one hand the number of lords who would have gone to fix a flooded ward themselves, rather than risk their people, and have three fingers and a thumb left. I don't think anyone back at the royal palace has ever been in water that deep if it wasn't a rose-scented bath and there were fifteen servants attending them."

"Don't be ridiculous. It takes at least twenty servants for a bath."

Another laugh, and Bedros tried not to feel so stupidly pleased. Why did he care about extracting laughs from a man he'd spent years hating?

Except he hadn't really hated Tellark. He'd just been told to hate him by Rocco and blindly obeyed.

Blinders removed, he saw a person he increasingly wished he'd had the sense to recognize as a potential real friend. Well, one more bitter regret for the pile, and the world moved on.

Speaking of the world moved on, at present it required movement from him. Forcing stiff limbs to work, he headed first for the warm bath that awaited him. Stripping off his sodden, half-frozen clothes he climbed into the hot water with a groan.

Macy came out of the wardrobe then, the drape that held his pins and needles still over one shoulder a bundle of fabric in his arms. "Oh, you're back, my apologies."

Bedros waved him off. "I can bathe myself when I must. Though if you could come put my hair back in order for me, I'd be grateful. My arms are still frozen and sore from all the chopping I did."

"Of course." He set aside his sewing and walked briskly across the room, gathering up a brush and other necessities from the vanity table as he did so.

Sitting on a stool at the head of the bath, he worked intently on brushing out Bedros's tangled hair, and then divided it into two braids that he then combined into an intricate set of knots at the back of his head. "All set, Your Grace."

"Thank you," Bedros said. "I can finish the rest, or pester my husband to help me."

"As you like." Macy departed, taking his sewing with him, and Bedros quickly finished bathing.

Heaving reluctantly out of the still-warm water, he dried off and went to pull on the clothes laid out on the bed. They were semi-formal, the clothes he would wear if he were hosting a banquet for the locals or attending one of the yearly fairs or festivals. It was definitely not the full formal attire he should be wearing to host a representative of the throne.

He could not wait to see Vare's face at the quiet insult.

Throughout, Tellark had remained silent, attention half-heartedly on a book he'd taken from the small collection of them Bedros kept in his room.

"How much time do you suppose has passed?" he asked.

Tellark glanced out the window. "Since you returned? Better part of an hour, I think."

"Good, plenty of time for Taniel to have finished writing up the documents we need."

"Won't they need our signatures?"

"I prefer not to ask questions that have uncomfortable answers."

Tellark's face clouded, but he snapped his

mouth shut on whatever he'd wanted to say.

Bedros flinched. "Sorry, poor jest. If I'd asked questions a long time ago, instead of just blithely not noticing, or not admitting, they needed to be asked, many things would be different."

"Yes, we might both already be dead, for a start." He heaved a sigh and stood. "Look, Akari—Bedros—I can't say I don't resent a lot of the things you said and did to me once, but my behavior wasn't always the best either, and there's plenty I regret. Whatever we might still need to work out and talk about, right now it's an impediment, and neither is it fair to keep judging you solely by what you used to be, instead of the person you've become. So let's leave off recriminations and snide comments for now, all right? If for no other reason than that this ruse will never work if we don't."

"It will take a lot more than letting bygones rest to convince Vare that we're so deeply in love we decided to risk life and limb to marry," Bedros replied. "You can't even remember to use my name."

Tellark smiled faintly. "Given the length to which an entire castle and village's worth of people—strangers—are going in order to save my life, the very least I can do is try just as hard. As I said before, you're hardly a fate worse than death, and at least a few steps above a pumpkin." He tilted his head, an exaggerated pensive look overtaking his face. "Not decided on oranges, though."

"A good orange is difficult to surpass," Bedros said, returning the smile. "You won't find those this far north, I'm afraid. Haven't seen one since I moved here. It's all apples, peaches, plums, and berry preserves around here—and whatever alcohol can possibly be made from them. Though the apples will be a memory if this war happens. We trade across the border for them. Usually beer for cider."

"I get the impression that alcohol is what drives the local economy."

"You're not wrong."

Tellark laughed.

There went that warm, pleased sensation again. Damn it. Please don't let him be going down the stupid, stupid path he feared he was.

"Though speaking of names, you should probably use mine. You've been calling me Tellark thus far." Tellark smirked. "Do you even know my given name?"

"Warren, of course," Bedros replied. "I remember it because I always wondered if anyone shortened it to 'Wren', like the bird, as a sort of play on 'Swallow's Nest.'"

That got him a nakedly startled look. "Uh. No. Everyone calls me Tellark, except my parents, who just used my name. I don't think any has ever shortened it."

"Really? Because they could also shorten Tellark to 'Lark' and just really go full heel on the bird theme. Lark, wren, swallow. Trio of songbirds."

Warren groaned. "Leave it to *you* to notice such a thing, when I have gone my whole life with no one, not even me, noticing it. You always were a brat."

"Everybody I know would agree with you. So which shall I make your pet name, darling? Wren or Lark?"

"I'm sure you'll find ways to use both," Warren replied. "What about you, any endearments I should know about?"

Bedros smiled faintly. "No. Like you, my parents simply used my name, and everyone else my surname. The only exception was my grandmother, who struggled with the language and always said my name 'bedrose' and shortened it to 'Rose' when I was a boy."

"A songbird and a rose, what a pair," Warren said, rolling his eyes. "It's so ridiculous and borderline maudlin it would *have* to mean we're telling the truth."

"You don't sound very affectionate, Wren."

Warren heaved a sigh. "Shall we go, then, before—"

A heavy pounding came at the door, even as a ruckus rose up as Bedros's guards clearly tried to deal with whoever Vare had sent to draw—or drag—him from his room.

"Good grief, can't a man spend some private time with his husband after a long, hard day?" Bedros smacked his forehead with his fingertips. "That reminds me." He strode into his wardrobe and combed through his jewelry chests, until he came up with what he needed.

Returning, he handed one ring and chain to Warren and slipped the other over his own head, where he hid it beneath his tunic.

"I prefer rubies," Warren said, running a thumb over the emerald ring Bedros had given him.

"I'll remember that for the real wedding," Bedros said, rolling his eyes. "These were all I had that match enough to be convincing."

"Speaking of being convincing…" Warren replied as he slipped his own fake wedding ring onto its chain and over his head, tucking it away like a secret beneath his layers.

"What?" Bedros frowned at the nervousness that seemed to have abruptly overtaken Warren, or maybe it had simply finally spilled over. "Is there something I haven't thought of?"

Finally standing, closing the book he'd still been holding with a snap and setting it aside, Warren crossed the room to stand in front of him, so close Bedros could smell sweat and a cologne made with amber and myrrh, and myriad spices he could not pick out. Mercy, did Warren always smell so good? How had he not noticed until now?

That was not a good direction for his thoughts to take.

He tried desperately to put them back on a wiser path, but the effort was ruined entirely when Warren moved in closer still, one of his hands slowly, hesitantly, coming up to brush back a strand of hair that had slipped the elaborate knotted braids. "Pet names won't convince anyone of anything if we're not comfortable being in one another's space."

Bedros's brows rose. "What are you suggesting?"

"Something stupid, so you should be fine," Warren replied, and that was all the warning Bedros got before he found himself being soundly, expertly kissed.

Well, then.

Bedros had never believed in refusing a good thing when it fell into his lap, and wasn't that a lovely image to torture himself with later. For the present, he slid his arms around Warren's waist and gave as good as he got. He couldn't remember the last time he'd kissed anyone—well, other than his almost-fiancée, when he'd been trying to do as told, but he hadn't enjoyed the kiss, and he'd loathed the idea of falling back into step for Rocco, so that had been that.

Warren tasted like wine, and a bit salty, his mouth warm, that tongue talented enough to melt Bedros's mind. If this was what it was like to kiss Warren when he still hated Bedros, how would it be if he could ever get Warren to like him?

Unfortunately, the thought was a bucket of cold water. Whatever Warren said about letting the past lie, he doubted there would ever be a day where Warren truly left behind every stupid fight, every shitty word, every hurtful moment between them, nearly all of them Rocco and Bedros's fault. No one fell in love with someone they hated; that was ballad nonsense.

He would remember this kiss, though, and rub it like salt in the wound of his regrets.

Breaking it off, he stepped back and struggled valiantly not to lick his lips. Great, now he knew what Warren looked like thoroughly kissed. Thoroughly kissed *by Bedros*. Gods above, how long had this been lurking, buried by Rocco's animosity and his stupid, blind obedience?

"What was that for?"

"So it looks like you were delayed by a predictable distraction," Warren said, his face giving none of his thoughts away, so vexing that Bedros wanted to scream. "Shall we? Before they break those doors down or someone gets stabbed?"

"I really don't care, as long as it's not my men, and they're much better at stabbing than Vare's soft city showpieces."

"He didn't bring the showpieces; he brought actual military, loaned from everyone's favorite General Stoneheart."

Bedros heaved a sigh and went to open the door. In the hallway, there was a sour standoff and at least two broken noses. "Enough. Stop assaulting my men. They're doing the job I told them to do. Tell Lord Vare I'm on my way."

Vare's guards, sure enough marked with the black and purple band of General Kara's troops, sulked off, nursing their broken noses and already-blackening eyes.

"Your Grace," said one of Bedros's guards. "I apologize for the disturbance."

"Hardly your fault Vare is an impatient ass. Thank you for putting up with them. Remain here, if you don't mind. I don't trust him not to have goons creeping around."

The men saluted, and with a last thank you, Bedros led the way back to the great hall.

Predictably, Vare was still standing around looming and glaring, a quartet of particularly ominous looking soldiers standing guard as though he were under threat of eminent assassination. They should all be so lucky.

As he took in Bedros's clothes, Vare looked like he wanted to do some assassinating of his own. Choosing to bide his time, or whatever, he simply said in frigid tones, "It's about time, Akari."

Bedros ignored him and headed for his usual table, where of course his wonderful, perfect, beloved staff already had dinner laid out, including pitchers of his favorite beer. Nerek, Kohar, and the others sat waiting, quietly drinking and very clearly having not invited Vare to join them. All around them, though, the other tables were strangely empty—all the stranger when half the village had so far been moved into the castle and the rest would be moved tomorrow. It could more than sustain that number; it had been built for such a thing, after all, but the great hall should be filled at supper time.

"Where are my people? Why are they not eating?"

"We have business to conduct, and I will not—"

"You have no authority here!" Bedros snarled. "How dare you keep my people from eating, or force them to eat in places that are cold and wet and ill-suited to it." He strode to the fire and picked up the mallet for the gong they almost never used. Striking it three times, setting the hall practically to vibrating with the force of the sound, he then went and took his seat. "Sit down, Vare, and say what you've come to say, or I will throw you out—and right into the moat, so help me."

Vare looked mad enough to spit fire, but as people trickled in, some carrying food they'd clearly been in the middle of eating already, others looking like they were miserably waiting their turn, he pinched his mouth together and strode across the room to join Bedros.

"Why are you sitting here?" he asked, looking around distastefully as they were quickly crowded in by everyone else, the noise growing exponentially. "Is this castle so backwater it can't provide a proper table for its lord?"

"I got rid of the table when I arrived. It took up valuable space and served no purpose beyond ego. But if the lack of a looming table is bruising your ego, which I know is fragile, feel free to take your leave." He poured beer for himself and Warren, pointedly not bothering for Vare. His guards loomed nearby, probably just as hungry as everyone else but not allowed to eat until Vare was asleep.

Vare looked ready to explode, his perpetually red face, a result of his excessive drinking and indulgence in other substances on occasion, grew nearly the very color of the flames in the nearby hearth. He poured himself a nearly-overflowing cup of wine, drank practically half of it, and then finally said, "I want to hear about this marriage, first of all. You can't expect me to believe such nonsense. The two of you? Married? Not even to save your own skins."

"He did save my life," Warren said quietly, the words barely audible in the din. He laid a hand over Bedros's on the table and twined their fingers together briefly. "That changed a lot of things—more than either of us ever expected. Whether you believe us or not is immaterial."

"It's quite material," Vare snapped. "Papers.

Now."

"Here, Your Grace," Taniel said from further down the table. "I pulled them from the archives as requested." He passed them down the table, but before Bedros could accept them, Vare snatched them up, pawing through them with hands he clearly hadn't bothered to wash after his arrival.

The look on his face, though, said that Taniel's work was as impeccable as promised. He threw them down in disgust, finished his wine, and poured a second brimming cup. Bedros signaled one of the attendants to bring more, praising himself for not rolling his eyes. Further down the table, his mages-in-residence were not quite so controlled.

He gave them a half-hearted admonishing look and sipped at his beer, flavored with blueberries and absolutely marvelous. Turning back to Vare, he said, "Satisfied? Would you be happier if we put the rings on?" He set his beer down and pulled out the ring he'd put on just minutes ago. "Do you need to inspect this as well?"

"When did you get to be such an ass, Akari?"

"You mean, when did I stop being a spineless dog for Rocco? When I woke up and realized our king was never the person I thought. What are you doing here? Clearly you haven't come to talk about the good old days."

Vare gave him a scathing look, and behind him his soldiers looked ready to quit. Hmmm. Maybe Kara's army wasn't as loyal as she and Vare thought. Something to look into, anyway. He'd set Nerek on it. "If your *husband* has come running frantically to your rescue, then we can stop playing games, Akari. You know damn good and well why I'm here."

"Oh, I'm not asking about the war you want to start. I'm just confused as to why you're bothering to come speak to me first. Would have been easier and faster to just begin the slaughter of your own people. Clearly someone agrees, given all the sabotage trying to weaken my castle and people in preparation for slaughter."

"You don't have to die with them, Akari. Rocco still has use for you, if you'd stop being a whiny child about everything." He cast Bedros a patronizing look he hadn't forgotten and definitely hadn't missed. "You can even pick a few favorites to spare alongside you. We're generous where we can be."

"Generous. You think you're *generous* by offering to save a handful of people from being murdered so Rocco can go to war? Let me guess: he's drained his coffers, and war is good business. It doesn't hurt that Serren has coastlines and other resources that we'd much rather have for free. You're not generous. You're a greedy, heartless ass and I'm ashamed I used to align myself with you and that craven bastard on the throne. Get out of my castle, Vare. If it's war you want, then it's war you shall have."

Further down the table, Nerek said, "Tell my mother I said hello."

So red in the face that Bedros half-expected him to pass out, Vare rose and stormed from the hall, his guards hastening to keep up with him.

Only minutes later, the guards on the curtain sent word he and his heavily-armed escort had departed—with shadows, as per Nerek's orders.

"That actually went better than I dared hope," Bedros said. "Well done on the paperwork, Tani."

Taniel smiled and bowed his head. "My pleasure."

"I swear you are the worst-behaved monk I have ever known," Kohar said. "Did you do anything in that monastery that you were supposed to? Or just all the things that broke the rules?"

"Little bit of both, to my regret and others," Taniel replied. "Shut up."

Kohar rolled his eyes, but when Nerek nudged him, stayed silent.

Next to Bedros, Warren smiled. He'd let go of Bedros's hand the moment Vare had vanished from sight, and Bedros hated how much he could still feel that touch. Probably he was just touch-starved. Seemed like he had been for most of his life. Had only himself to blame, though, so moving on. "I have to say, Bedros, that could have been handled more tactfully, but I enjoyed it immensely. Don't think I've ever seen someone get to Vare that way. People are far too scared of him."

"They've clearly never seen him behind closed doors, cowering and whining and slavering to Rocco. He's like one of those thorny buds that grow all over the royal city. They look vicious, and the thorns can hurt a bit, but when you rip the stupid things open all you get is white fluff quickly scattered by the wind."

"Thorny reeds." Warren laughed. "What a perfect description. The next time I'm in the area, I'll have to ensure it spreads all over town. He'll never live it down."

"Just don't give me credit. I have enough problems right now."

"I like to think I'm a kinder husband than that."

Bedros bit off saying something sappy or stupid—probably it would be both—and only smiled. "Everyone knows I'm the one who married above my station here, whatever the titles. I just hope this works, and you're not hurt more than you already have been by giving up essentially your entire life."

Warren shrugged. "I made my decision fully aware of the consequences. I'll face the fallout. I'm grateful, though, to you and yours for doing so much to help me."

Chuckling softly, Bedros lifted his cup. "We seem to have a knack for saving each other, despite a history that says we'd prefer to do otherwise. A peculiar trend, but I rather like it. Enough talking, though. Let's eat now that we can enjoy it."

He smacked his spoon against his glass until silence fell across the hall and made swift work of thanking everyone for their cooperation, and assuring them all would be well and that they should come to him with any problems—immediately if an emergency, otherwise he'd hold audience all morning to attend matters.

With so many people, it would probably be all morning and afternoon, but whatever was necessary, he would do.

For the moment, though, he was going to enjoy his meal, and that he was sharing it with a man who once would have been perfectly happy to see him dead right alongside Rocco and Vare.

By the time dinner ended, everyone was in a much better mood, which was all Bedros could have asked for. Whatever problems they were facing, the greater burden of them should be on no shoulders but his.

When he'd finished the last of his beer, he dragged himself to his feet. "I suppose I should be off to bed, so I'm awake bright and early for whatever Vare and his cronies throw at us next."

To his surprise, Warren rose with him, hooking an arm through his. "Ending the night early, are we, husband?" His smirk made the double entendre clear, to the delighted laughter of the entire hall.

Bedros rolled his eyes, but smiled in reply. "There won't even be a beginning if you keep that up."

They departed chased by laughter and ribald comments, and it was all too easy to believe, for a single, brief, bittersweet moment, that this was his life—a loving husband, happy people, not a single care in the world.

Truth returned in the next breath, of course, but Bedros left the old wounds to deal with later. For the present, he simply enjoyed Warren on his arm, the smile that lingered on his face, despite the fact he must hate everything about his current situation.

They walked in silence for a couple of minutes, until they were in the quieter portions of the castle, and Warren asked, "So how do you spend your days when they're not in upheaval?"

"How does any noble spend his days? I read reports, I hold audience to deal with problems, I ride about the territory as weather permits, so on and so forth. Surely it's not so different at your end of the kingdom?"

"No, it's not, actually, save that I spend some of my days on boats, though normally my presence is far too required for me to isolate myself thus. I hadn't thought I'd care for your colder climes, but I can see the appeal they would hold for those who can endure the cold, even if I've not been here very long."

Bedros smiled. "Wait until it snows. Everything here revolves around winter, so while the rest of the world sleeps in the cold, in the mountains we thrive. Which reminds me…" His smiled dropped. "You have perhaps a couple of weeks before you're essentially snowbound for the season."

"I knew what I was getting into, as much as anyone can. I didn't come here blindly."

"I know, but people who come here thinking they're prepared often realize they're not remotely ready for being snowed into a single place for months on end. This year is going to be especially bad. It's entirely possible we won't be able to leave the keep, let alone the grounds, for weeks at a time."

"Still sounds, broadly at least, more survivable than being becalmed for days on end. We were nearly out of food, stuck in the doldrums, when the wind at last picked up again. I think seafaring has at least as many stories of humans eating their fellows as your mountains. Strange the things we have in common, when our worlds are so drastically different."

"Survival can swiftly turn into a grim undertaking anywhere," Bedros said softly as they reached the door to Warren's room. "Though I did not mean for our conversation to turn so grim."

"I'm used to my husband's strange turns of conversation," Warren replied with a laugh, and gave the barest tug of his arm, keeping them both moving toward Bedros's room.

Inside, doors closed behind them, Warren let go and went to sit in a nearby chair, sprawling out with a sigh. "That went far better than I could have hoped. Bravo to you and yours."

"'Mine' never mind getting into a bit of mischief," Bedros replied. "It's the very least we owe you, at any rate, for saving our lives. Especially mine, when no one would blame you for being more than happy to leave me for dead."

"You did save *my* life."

"We both know I was Rocco's faithful lackey who did whatever he said. Saving your life is the very least I owe you."

Warren gave him a pensive look. "Why were you so devoted to him? I never understood it. Answer me that."

Bedros sighed and went to sit on the bench at the foot of his bed, setting to work on the laborious process of taking down his hair and preparing it for sleeping. "I was a poor boy suddenly turned new wealth boy. My reception into the world of nobility was not kind. I was sneered at, mocked, beaten… I endured many a night of bruises and bloodied nose. No matter how hard I tried, I could not seem to find where and how to fit into a world I'd never been meant for. Then along came Rocco. Charming, friendly. Showed me around. How to talk. How to dress. He was a prince, and I was a lowly farmer boy, and he wanted *me* to be his closest friend. Who wouldn't fall for that?"

He stared down at his hands. "By the time I was willing to admit to myself the mess I was in, the mistakes I had made, it was too little too late. I ended as I began: alone and out of place. I am sorry you and so many others were victims of my stupidity and obliviousness. Looking back, it's painfully clear all the real friends I could have had, the life I could have built, if I hadn't been so stupid as to fall for Rocco's manipulations."

"You're not to blame for being the victim of a man all too good at doing precisely what he did to you," Warren replied.

"I'm responsible for my own actions, and there were plenty of them, each one heinous. Fights, ugly words… my list of crimes goes on and on."

"Remorse and doing better aren't to be dismissed," Warren said quietly. "I'm not going to lie. I came here expecting to find the pompous lackey I knew for years. Prepared to do whatever was necessary to make you listen to me about the threat coming down on you. Yet I can find no trace of the bastard who once nearly broke my nose in a drunken brawl or managed to upend an entire bowl of punch on me at my niece's betrothal ball. All I've encountered since my arrival is a good lord dearly loved by his people."

The words were a twisting, bittersweet ache in Bedros's chest. A sharp reminder of all he could have been, and had, if he hadn't been so fucking stupid. "Well, it's good to hear that I am, in fact, learning from my mistakes. Though you're still suffering for them."

"Enough. I'm a man grown; I make my own decisions. My friends and family are removed from danger, and nothing would be gained by harming my tenants and leaving the land and fishing boats they work to languish. The worst that's happened so far is that I'm to be snowed in with my surprise husband for a few months." He made a face. "Well, and likely a bloody battle, but I'm still hoping we can avert that somehow."

"Let's hope." Bedros finished braiding his hair for the night, tied it off with a bit of leather, and went to go change out of his fancy clothes. By the time he stepped out of his dressing room, he'd expected to be alone.

Instead, he was greeted by the sight of a bare-chested Warren in his bed—looking right at home in his bed. It was only then that Bedros noticed all of Warren's belongings had been moved to his room as well. "Playing the long game, are we?"

"I would not put it past Vare to try to surprise us with a midnight or pre-dawn visit, just to catch us in a lie."

"Very well, but if you try to hog the blankets I'm shoving you right onto the floor."

Warren laughed. "I'll try to behave."

Bedros had never wanted someone to misbehave more in his life, but he bit his tongue on saying so and simply doused the lights before climbing into bed. He shifted restlessly for a few minutes, far from used to sharing space with someone and not quite sure how to go about it.

As a young boy, he'd slept in the main room of the cabin with the other children and the staff; his parents had possessed the only bedroom in the house, and it hadn't been much larger than a storage space. When they'd suddenly had a house where he had a room all to himself, and that room nearly the size of their old house, he hadn't known what to do with it all.

Over the years, he'd gotten used to sleeping alone. Strange that now it was *not* sleeping alone that threw him off balance. In the end, he settled far to the edge, one arm beneath him, the heavy blankets pulled up high and wrapped snuggly. They'd be warmer if he drew the curtains around the bed, but being closed in that way always made him feel like he was suffocating or like there was someone wandering his room that he couldn't see.

The silence was strange, even oppressive, but if he tried to break it he'd just make things more awkward, knowing him. Instead he just closed his eyes and tried to distract himself with all he'd need to do come morning, the inventory inspections that would need to be done before rain turned to snow, the hunt for a certain slimy ex-monk…

"You're so tense you're vibrating," Warren said, and Bedros nearly squeaked in surprise and alarm as a hand curled around his upper arm, and Warren was suddenly all but pressed up against his back. In the dark, his husky voice took on a sultry note that did nothing whatsoever to make Bedros *less* tense. "Something wrong?"

"It's been a strange day."

Warren chuckled. "I'll concede that. If I'm making you uncomfortable, I can sleep on the floor or in the dressing room or something."

"No!" Bedros turned, alarmed—and forgot until they collided just how close Warren was now. "You'd freeze to death. It may only be autumn, but the temperatures are starting to dip into freezing at night. You're fine. I didn't mean for my restlessness to keep you awake. If anyone should sleep—"

"Shut up, Bedros," Warren said, and kissed him.

If Bedros had been given a hundred guesses as to what Warren would do after telling him to shut up, he wouldn't have suggested kissing even as a jest. Everything in him railed this was a bad idea, but damn it, for just a few moments he wanted to enjoy *what could have been.*

He kissed Warren back with everything he should have had the sense to realize when they'd first met. They'd been younger and stupider, but even then there were things about Warren he should have noticed properly, instead of letting Rocco warp his perceptions and turn a real friend into an enemy. It would never stop hurting, but he sensed if it did, he'd be right back where he started.

Drawing back, Warren said, "When I said shut up, I meant in your own head too, Bedros."

"Forgive me for being a bit startled by this turn of events."

"Whatever. I know when someone wants to fuck me, and you've never been hard on the eyes yourself. The first time I saw you, I wanted you. Then you proved to be an ass. How about instead of going out of our way to make one another miserable, the way we have all our lives, we try doing the complete opposite for once? We're adults, theoretically. We can act like it, now and later."

"That would have to be a very generous

theoretically," Bedros said with a laugh, and this time was not held back by doubts and self-loathing when Warren resumed kissing him. He was a hells of a kisser, and still tasted faintly of beer and the sweets they'd had before ending the evening.

He went easily when Warren rolled him onto his back and pushed him deep into the bedding, sliding a leg between his thighs and pinning his wrists. Bedros laughed breathlessly. "Something you want, Wren?"

In the flickering light of the fire, he could just see the hint of a smirk curving Warren's delectable mouth. "Are your wants in conflict?"

"I should think it's pretty obvious they're not."

Warren resumed the kisses, but this time didn't stop at Bedros's mouth. He continued on down, leaving a trail of fire as he went, searing marks on his jaw and throat and chest, where he added some teasing nips for good measure. Throughout, Bedros tried to do some touching of his own, but Warren's grip on his wrists was firm, and it was pretty clear the current arrangement was *do as you're told,* and it was not the lord of the castle who was in charge.

He'd never really had a problem with that.

"These are in the way," Warren said, and Bedros groaned at the husky tone of his voice before he was freed so Warren could put both hands to work removing the loose pants Bedros had drawn on to sleep Normally, he was happy to sleep naked, but he'd worried something would happen in the dead of night and had wanted to be prepared.

He gasped and writhed as his pants were cast away and he was bared fully to the chilly night air—and Warren's heated gaze. Then a calloused hand wrapped around his cock and Bedros could think about nothing but *want* and *need* and *right now damn it.*

Some of that he must have vocalized, because

Warren let out a positively smug chuckle before shifting his position and putting that mouth to work in ways that had Bedros moaning and begging within moments. He gripped Warren's hair with one hand, holding it tightly but careful not to yank, as Warren took him deep, sucked hard, that tongue running up and down the length of his cock with delightful skill.

Just before he came, though, trembling and aching and desperately needing, Warren pulled back and wiped his mouth with the back of one hand. "I want you to come on my cock. Where is your bed oil?"

"Bastard," Bedros replied with a whimpering moan. "I was perfectly capable of doing that without the torture first."

"Sucking your cock is torture?"

"You know exactly what I mean!" Bedros groaned again as he forced himself up and went to fetch the oil that he seldom bothered to keep by the bed, because on the rare occasion he indulged in getting himself off, mostly it just left him feeling lonelier than ever.

He'd barely reached the bed when he was dragged roughly into it and put on all fours.

"Not going to lie, Bedros, I like having you wholly at my mercy for once."

Bedros tried to reply to that, but the slick finger Warren pushed roughly into him shattered every thought in his head. He couldn't remember the last time someone else had touched him, let alone so intimately. Bedros moaned and rested his head on his folded arms, spreading as much as he could, begging with every fiber of his body for more.

Warren seemed more than happy to give it, as one finger rapidly progressed to three, leaving Bedros almost mad with want before the fingers withdrew and were replaced by Warren's long, hard cock.

After that, it was all sensation: thrusting and groaning, the slap of skin and panting breaths, sweat stinging his eyes and soaking the nape of his neck, making the fine linen sheets stick to his skin. He was overheated and overstimulated, and barely had the wherewithal to muffle his scream as he finally came apart, unable to hold back a second longer.

Warren was still fucking him as he slowly came down from the mind-shattering release, but Bedros had always kind of liked that, feeling his companion still going, still hard and needing and eager, leaving him overstimulated and wrung out.

When Warren finally came, Bedros's cock tried to rise to the occasion, but that was entirely too ambitious.

He collapsed on the bed, sprawled haphazardly, as Warren withdrew. "Why *aren't* you married? Someone should have had the sense to snap you a long time ago."

Warren chuckled, heavy and slow, sleep clearly getting the better of him after what must have been an extremely long day. "I've had offers. Even considered it once or twice. But none of them ever… I don't know… felt right. Guess I'm too picky for my own good."

"Of course you are," Bedros said with a laugh of his own. "You were always very clear and precise about your wants. Rocco hated that about you, and I dutifully followed suit."

"I like you better away from him," Warren said around a yawn, the words fading off, and only moments later he was fast asleep, snoring softly, a gentle counterpoint to the crackling fire and the drumming rain outside.

Though it sounded like it might have turned to sleet. That would make the morning interesting. Bedros sighed and rose, and quickly got the bedding sorted out, careful all the while not to wake Warren.

When the bed was once more clean and dry, he crawled under the blankets already warmed by Warren and, this time, had no trouble settling in to sleep.

Unfortunately, he hadn't been asleep long, to judge by the fire, when a pounding at the door woke him. Bedros opened his eyes, pinched them shut, then willed them open again. "Come in," he called hoarsely, then cleared his throat and tried again.

The door flew open to admit Nerek, dressed for war and looking pissed enough to fight the whole thing by himself. There were reasons Bedros paid him significantly more than was typical for his position. "My scouts have reported movement in the enemy encampments. Small groups preparing to move out."

"Ambush and sabotage," Bedros replied, and Nerek nodded, face grim.

General Kara was setting out to cause mass chaos and hysteria. From there, it would be easy to do a great deal of slaughtering and have the matter conclude to their favor. Likely with nobody left alive who could contradict them. Like every single person in the castle who'd heard him bickering with Vare last night, and all the people across the border who'd learned of what was going on from soldiers who couldn't keep their mouths shut as instructed.

"Macy, get my trunk," he said as Macy appeared from the room off Bedros's where he slept. "Nerek, see my horse is readied."

"You're not going out there yourself," Nerek said. "That's the definition of stupid."

"It's the definition of my position."

Nerek scowled. "You're not a fighter. You'll just be a liability."

From near the bed, where he'd climbed out and

was fetching his discarded clothes, Warren laughed loudly. "You think *Bedros* can't fight? Bedros, what in the world have you been doing around here that they think you're *that* useless?"

Bedros rolled his eyes. "I mean, I certainly can't fight *well* these days, but I still remember how to clobber people."

Nerek gave him a confused look. Warren just laughed harder as he went over to his own trunks, threw them open, and began removing items—armor, weapons, all the other bits required of going into battle. "That's how we met," he said, glancing briefly at Nerek over his shoulder. "In training. He beat the shit out of me, and afterward when we were done…"

"I was an ass, because Rocco had convinced me you were a greater ass," Bedros said flatly. "I drove you away, instead of making a real friend." He turned away, focusing on his breathing, on the matter before him, not on all the bitter, aching regrets of his past.

As Macy dragged the heavy trunk from the storeroom, Bedros fetched the key for it. He unlocked the trunk, threw back the lid, and stared tiredly at the armor and weapons carefully stowed within it. He hadn't bothered to retain his heavy plate mail—that would be suicide in these mountains in winter. He had kept the leather armor and the chainmail, though, and all his swords, daggers, and more, though some of them were stored elsewhere due to size.

He and Macy set to work, and in a matter of minutes, Bedros was dressed for battle. The clothes were strange after being ignored for so long, but still familiar too.

Nerek shook his head. "Come on, then. I sent someone about your horse. Should be ready by now."

Warren joined them, equally dressed for war, and entirely too good looking about it, and they headed off.

Outside, the rain had indeed turned to sleet at some point, leaving the whole world dark, cold, and treacherous. Bedros settled his heavy fur-trimmed wool cloak around him, pulled up his cowl, and mounted his horse. Nerek, Kohar, Corsair, Taniel, and Warren formed a loose circle around him. "Nerek, you and I are taking the bulk of our forces to the border. No one and nothing is to cross it. Kohar, Taniel, each of you go with a team into the village and surrounding farms, see what you can do to mitigate whatever our old buddy Vosgi is up to. Warren, join Corsair's team, man scouts and patrols around the keep. Everyone be careful."

"*You* be careful," Nerek said.

"Since when do you even know which end of the sword is which?" Kohar asked.

Bedros laughed. Warren laughed louder.

"Move out," Bedros replied, and heeled his horse into action. She snorted, breath misting in the air, and took off easily, clearly aware this was no ordinary jaunt. She probably recognized the armor and sword, the familiar mood of a looming fight. They might both have settled since moving to Rehm, but they hadn't entirely lost their edges yet.

He let Nerek take the lead, more than content to simply ride along with him, leaving the soldiers to their business. He was there to deal with the inevitable castellan and general, not tell Nerek how to do his job.

The sleet made the going slow and dangerous. Twice soldiers went sliding, and it was the gods alone that spared the horses from taking some fatal injury.

Eventually, though, they cleared the first portion of the forest and the border wall—

Fire erupted, scaring everyone, sending all the horses save Nerek and Bedros's into a panic. One horse flat out took off back toward home.

Bedros drew his sword and headed for what had seemed to be the source—right as soldiers poured out from all sides. Well, hardly surprising they'd been expected, and there were only so many paths that could be taken this time of year if one wanted to survive the journey.

He slashed at one of the soldiers who came at him, catching the bastard on his poorly-protected forearm, then moving in for a killing blow. Wheeling his horse around, he attacked two more who weren't bothering to watch their backs.

After that, it all got too chaotic to keep straight. Hack. Slash. Stab. Kick. Dismount to take care of a few stragglers. Seek out the source of the fire that was still trying to take hold of the wet, half-frozen forest.

By the time the fight was ended, and the fire well and truly extinguished, Bedros was ready to go back to bed and stay there through winter. Instead he wiped his face, roughly cleaning it of blood, sweat, and melting sleet, and looked to Nerek. "Any losses?"

"Two injured, one horse down."

"Send the injured back, the rest of us carry on."

"Sir." Nerek spun away and set to work spreading the orders, and they were shortly on their way again.

They made it the rest of the way to the border wall without incident, to be greeted by a veritable wall of soldiers on the other side of it, just visible through the iron gate, every last one of their faces grim.

A woman strode up to the gate, face drawn, brown skin washed out in the flickering light of lanterns and torches. "Akari."

"Janell. I'm sorry for all this."

"You're not to blame for politicians playing their stupid games. Just so long as it's clear we have no interest in war."

"Neither do I—neither does anyone else in this damned kingdom, save those who stand to profit from it. We're doing our best to stop it, but they want a bloodbath."

"I that's what they want, there's no price too high to get it," Janell replied grimly. "No one is using us to start a war, damn it. We're ready for them, and I've already sent on letters, signed and sealed, to ensure word of this gets out if the worst comes to pass."

Bedros nodded. "If you can hold the gate, then, we'll return to the village and see what we can do there."

"Of course. Go."

Nerek left several of their own soldiers there to assist, though hopefully it would come to nothing except a lot of standing around in the miserable weather.

They headed back to the village, braced for another attack but thankfully encountering nothing.

Probably because when the village came into view, everything was chaos. Fire. Screaming. Crying. People running in all directions.

Rage filled Bedros, and a hate like nothing he'd ever felt before. His people had bothered *no one*. Their biggest 'crime' was an enthusiastic unsanctioned trade agreement in all things relating to alcohol with their northern neighbors. Yet here they were being slaughtered so wealthy people in cozy palaces could make more money than they would ever spend.

He plunged into the chaos, sword drawn, and started hacking and slashing his way through. It was anguishing, having to cut down his own countrymen, but they were the ones who'd started this, who'd chosen to betray their own.

The knights went first, though he wasn't properly equipped to deal with them; he hadn't thought

Kara would risk so many horses in the treacherous weather. But why would a woman like that care about horses where she didn't care about people?

Eventually one of them succeeded in removing him from his saddle, sending Bedros slamming-tumbling down into the very heart of the chaos. He regained his feet and braced for the knight coming at him, hefting a fallen bit of timber from a ruined house to serve as a makeshift polearm.

He knocked the bastard right out, and made swift work of him after that. Then he turned to the next fight, and the next, and the next.

By the time the movement stopped, he was soaked head to foot in sweat, blood, and substances he preferred not to look at long enough to figure them out. He yanked off his helmet and threw it aside, wiping sweat and blood from his face as best he could with a relatively clean bit of sleeve. "Where is Nerek?"

It took a few minutes, but eventually the answer came back to him. "He's at the south end, by the laundress's hut."

"Thank you." Still gripping his sword, nowhere near calmed down enough to clean and sheath it, Bedros headed off through the bloody aftermath of battle to find Nerek.

Each dead body, each wounded, each terrified man, woman, and child just fed his anger, resurrected things he'd tried to leave behind when he'd been given a second chance with his exile.

By the laundress's hut, Nerek had several prisoners bound and staked to the ground for extra security and was interrogating them relentlessly.

Nearby Kohar was slumped against a wall, clearly dead on his feet, just as filthy as the rest of them, the knot he'd put his hair in fallen to one side of his head like some strange, flopped over hat. His left arm was bandaged and in a sling, cradled against his chest. "Are you all right?"

"Been better, been worse," Kohar replied. "Taniel made all the difference. He might have illicit knowledge, but it's proven to be damned useful knowledge. He's out helping the wounded right now. I'd gladly do the same, but I'm depleted, and I wanted to stay here in case Nerek needed something."

"Of course. What is he trying to get out of them?"

"My mother," Nerek replied, turning away from the prisoners. "I was headed right for her, but she broke rank like a fucking coward and ran. Didn't even call for a retreat, just left her people to die so she could make a clean getaway."

"Where is Vare?"

"Being brought," Nerek said flatly.

"Good. I want him in the square, and General Kara too when you find her. People deserve justice and closure."

"Yes, Your Grace," Nerek replied. "Corsair is getting the report for you. I'll send him to the square to see you."

"Thank you, Captain. For everything."

Nerek nodded and turned back to the prisoners.

Bedros made his way back through the village, moving more slowly this time, helping with the wounded and various problems as best he could along the way, delegating as needed.

By the time he finally made it to the square, a small crowd had assembled and was steadily growing.

In the center, shackled to old iron loops in the ground that were rarely used anymore, save for unruly livestock, was Vare.

"You can't do this to me!" Vare snarled, full of hate and fury as he glared at Bedros. "I am the Royal

Castellan, voice of His Royal Majesty King—"

"We all know who you are and who the king is, thank you," Bedros said. "We're country folk, not simpletons. Contrary to popular thought, there *is* a difference." He beckoned a soldier forward and handed off his sword. "Sharpen that, or bring me one that's already sharp. *Very* sharp. If you can find a saber, all to the better."

"Yes, Your Grace." The soldier was young, but to judge by the brief widening of his eyes before he regained himself, he had enough experience to know why Bedros would make such a request.

Vare, of course, was oblivious. Or at least too busy with his offended ego to care about the truly important matters. "If you don't unhand me right this minute, Akari, I will see to it—"

"See to it, what?" Bedros asked. "That we suffer? You've already slaughtered at least half my guards. If the vast majority of my people hadn't already been moved to the castle, there wouldn't be any of them left—and still many of them are dead. All because you and Rocco don't have enough power and money. I'm not having it. If you wanted to slaughter me and mine, you should have chosen a less cowardly general. Now instead of being the messenger, you're going to be the message."

Finally, Vare seemed to realize the truth of his predicament. "W-w-what are you talking about?"

Bedros didn't reply, simply waited as the soldier he'd sent out came running back bearing a sheathed saber. Right behind him was Nerek and several guards, hauling General Kara, bound in chains. They deposited her right next to Vare and secured her to the same iron loops.

Drawing the saber and casting the sheath aside, Bedros said, "Well, now I have to decide if one message will suffice, or if I should send two."

"You don't have the spine," Kara hissed. "If you did, you'd still be one of us, instead of out here playing at country squire like some pathetic worm."

"I think you don't know what courage looks like, and you couldn't muster it to save your own life. Enough chatter."

Around them, the crowd had grown significantly, large enough that people must have come down from the keep. Including Warren, who stood watching solemnly.

Bedros turned his attention to Nerek. "You should leave."

Nerek shook his head. "No, She made her choices. She ceased to be my mother a long time ago. I have to burn friends tonight. I'm staying."

"As you wish." Bedros faced Vare and Kara. "You'd best hope the gods are kinder to you than you were to anyone here on earth. Any last words?"

"You'll hang for this," Vare snarled. "Rocco would never—"

It had been a long time since Bedros had done anything as vicious and nasty as behead someone, but his body remembered the movements, how to do it in a single, clean cut. Vare's head went tumbling, and he turned to Kara, whose skin had gone ashen. "You, General? Any last words?"

"I have always served king and country."

"You're meant to serve the people," Bedros said, and finished her as swiftly as he had Vare. Then he threw the sword aside and knelt, taking several deep breaths until his stomach calmed and he no longer wanted to scream.

He hadn't missed this. Any of it. He especially hadn't missed all the fucking violence. He'd never understand people like Kara, who seemed to thrive on it.

He liked being the peaceful, quiet Duke of Rehm. Why couldn't they just leave him the hells alone?

A gentle hand wrapped around his arm and helped him to his feet. Bedros smiled wanly at Warren. "That's that, I guess, other than delivering the message."

"We'll sort out the details in the morning."

Bedros nodded and headed off with him to help with the wounded, the dead, and all the destruction that would need to be cleaned up.

*~*~*

It took three days to clean up the mess, prepare pyres for their fallen, and hold the ceremony.

The royal soldiers, Bedros simply made sure to get a list of their names, personal effects that should be returned to family or other loved ones, and then had people cart them up the mountain to the Bone Field, a rocky plateau where bodies that couldn't be burned, or which didn't deserve a pyre, were left for the elements and animals to take care of.

The only exception were the severed heads of Vare and Kara, which Bedros set some hunters to preserving for him.

He was reviewing the list of the dead and their belongings one last time when the heads were brought to him. Two village hunters, in the leathers and myriad weapons and tools that marked their trade, strode into the hall carrying wooden crates, and behind them came a young man with the lids to the crates.

"Your Grace," said one of the hunters.

"Kira, Bartin, thank you," Bedros said, handing the papers off to the woman who'd been helping him go through everything. He motioned for them to set the crates on one of the tables. "Let's see them, then, so I know exactly what I'm sending to His Majesty."

Solemnly, the two hunters obeyed, and withdrew the cloths that had been protecting the contents until the lids could be nailed on. Reaching into the creates, they each withdrew the heads within.

Each head had been meticulously preserved: the eyes, tongues, and other inner bits removed and the whole stuffed with dressed flax before the eyes, mouth, and severed neck were sewn shut. After that, they had been steamed, then carefully roasted, bathed in oil to keep the skin from blackening. Next was smoking, followed by the final dressing. The hunters had done their job so well, the features were preserved near-perfectly.

His Majesty would have no problems identifying his steward and general.

"Pack them up," he said, and motioned for his nearby clerk to pay the hunters for their grisly task.

When they'd gone again, he returned to his lists, working for another two hours before he was satisfied each person and precious belonging was accounted for. Handing the papers off to Velle, the woman who'd been helping him, he said, "See everything is loaded into the carts, sign off when its done, and leave the papers in my office. Let me know if there are any problems."

"Your Grace." She bowed and swept out of the room, followed by a couple of people she signaled to assist her.

Bedros stretched and groaned, and sat down rubbing the back of his sore neck. It would turn into a headache if he wasn't careful, and that was the very last thing he needed.

"You look ready for bed."

The words, said in Warren's husky voice, sent tingles down Bedros's spine. While Warren had slept with him every night, those nights had been full of hard sleep, both of them too exhausted to do much more than mumble goodnight as they fell over.

Not that Bedros would have presumed a repeat of their one time together. He'd never expected that much. Given it was the one bright spot in a flood of blood and violence… well, he was sure Warren could not wait to be away from Rehm for good.

A fool could hope, though, and Bedros was nothing if not a fool.

He smiled tiredly as Warren settled next to him at the table. "I think after these past many days we could all stand to stay abed for an equal number. Alas, too much to do." He reached out unthinking to wipe away a trace of ash from Warren's cheek. "How goes the clean-up."

"So close to finished they didn't need or want me around anymore," Warren said with a laugh. "I must look a fright if you're trying to clean me."

Bedros hated the way his face burned. "Hardly, and you damn well know it, Wren."

Warren's eyes glittered with something Bedros hadn't ever expected to see, let alone twice. "I'm enjoying getting compliments from you. Keep it up and I'll give you a generous farewell tonight."

Bedros hated infinitely more the way his heart dropped into his stomach like a stone into a well. Warren hadn't been here long, and most of his stay had frankly been miserable, but he already felt like a part of Castle Rehm. "I like parts of that sentence, and dislike other parts."

That got him a laugh. "You don't want me to fuck you, then? And you do want me to leave?"

"Stop being an ass, Warren," Bedros said, and leaned in to kiss him, realizing too late how stupid that was, that Warren may not appreciate being kissed right there in the open where anyone and everyone could see.

Before he could withdraw and apologize, though, Warren gripped his hair tightly in one hand and held him in place, kissing him like Bedros was his property and served at his pleasure. Or maybe Bedros was letting his own preferences run away with him. Whatever. Warren could kiss, and Bedros would enjoy each and every one, to savor when Warren was gone.

When they finally drew apart, Bedros could not remember what they'd been talking about or what he'd been planning on doing next.

Smirking, as if realizing the effect he'd had, Warren withdrew and thanked the flustered servant who came up with plates of food and a pitcher of beer.

"I assume you'll want to leave at first light?"

"If not sooner," Warren said with a sigh. "I don't want to leave when it feels like there's still so much to do, but somebody must play the grim messenger, and I am best positioned to do so."

Bedros didn't reply immediately, as the smaller door to the hall opened and Nerek came blowing in like the frigid wind that followed him. Kohar came in a few paces behind him, covered head to foot in mud like he'd fallen into the biggest possible puddle he could find.

"Dare I ask?" Bedros said as they approached.

Kohar rolled his eye. "No. I'm going to get cleaned up." He stomped off, chased by aggravated servants trying to mitigate the damage to their floors.

Nerek took a seat across from them, setting his sword on the bench beside him. "He slipped and fell. It was hilarious. The rebuilding is going relatively well, all things considered, and I've got my people patrolling, but I don't think we'll have further trouble. Any soldiers we didn't kill are back at their camp and staying there until you give the order they're allowed to return home."

Bedros sighed. "Soon, though I'm sure holding them has come to nothing. There's always at least one who slips away." He took a swallow of his beer and turned a brief glance on Warren. "Are you certain you want to take up the role of messenger?"

"Someone has to, and I'm not going to leave the job to someone His Majesty could kill with little consequence. We're still married, after all." Warren smiled faintly. "Killing me at this point would do him more harm than good, especially with the gifts I'll be delivering."

"I'd still feel better if you weren't going alone."

"I'll go with him," Nerek said. "I have to attend to my mother's estate anyway. Kohar isn't very happy with me, but it makes sense. Just would you two try to stay out of trouble while I'm gone?"

Bedros laughed before he drank more beer. "I'm not even going to pretend to make that promise."

Nerek rolled his eyes and Warren laughed.

Setting his cup down, Bedros said, "You said the reconstruction was going well? Did the workers have estimates on when everything will be finished and people can move back to their homes? I don't mind a full castle, but I'm sure most of these people are damned tired of sleeping on the floor and would like their normal routines back."

"A couple more weeks. The fire damage was extensive, and this damned weather helps nothing. They had to stop twice today because of the sleet, and it's going to be dark soon, so that's yet another day lost. But what hours they had, they made the most of."

Bedros nodded, making a mental note to see they were paid generously. "The heads are ready, and my dear husband wants to leave first thing in the morning."

"All right. I'd better go break the news to

Kohar." Rolling his eyes, but also smiling like the besotted, adoring lover he was, Nerek rose, grabbed his sword, and strode off.

There was a burst of laughter across the hall, closer to the fire, where Taniel was telling stories to children who ranged in age from three or so up to nearly adulthood. Even a few nearby adults, working on laying out supper and tidying up the hall, seemed drawn in. Leaning against the wall, one leg up, arms crossed over his chest, Corsair was doing more listening—and looking—than his actual job of overseeing the hall.

Bedros could commiserate. He looked his fill of Warren whenever he got the barest chance to do so.

Pushing away his empty plate, Warren swung his legs over the long bench seat and rose. "You should come help me pack."

"You don't even do your own packing, why would you need—" Bedros stopped at the look on Warren's face. "I'm a dumbass. Of course I'll come help you pack. Though I don't know why you're pretending to be coy or subtle."

"It's called flirting, Bedros."

Not really sure how to respond to that, not sure he could in a way that wouldn't be pathetic or depressing or both, Bedros simply rose and walked with him out of the hall. His skin practically tingled with anticipation, hot sparks dancing along his spine, and his cock was already trying its best to humiliate him on the short trip upstairs to his chambers.

The door had barely closed behind them when Warren fisted a hand in his shirt and dragged/shoved Bedros to his knees. "Do I need to spell out the instructions?"

Bedros didn't whimper, but it was a near thing. "Someone has gotten bold and bossy."

"You have no idea how many times I wanted to

see you exactly like this." Warren smiled wryly. "Some of the fantasies were nicer than others."

Bedros really didn't care about the details, though imagining each and every one did nothing to cool his ardor. "Did you want to tie me down and beat my ass for being an odious bastard, Wren? I didn't know you had it in you."

Warren's eyes glittered with want and promise as he curled a hand into Bedros's hair and yanked hard, leaving the knot he'd put it in completely ruined. He shoved Bedros's face into his crotch. "Put that bratty mouth of yours to better use."

Chuckling, Bedros reached up to unlace Warren's hose and pull out his cock, thick and hard and demanding attention. The fingers in his hair tightened again, all the warning he got before Warren was using his mouth, thrusting in and out, going so deep Bedros's eyes watered. He took it all gladly, though, sucking hard, tongue running over whatever he could reach. He glanced up through his lashes whenever he could manage it, loving the heat in Warren's eyes as he stared back. Loving more the way he finally looked away, eyes closing, as his climax tore through him, spilling hot and salty down Bedros's throat.

He pulled slowly off Warren's cock, and wiped spittle and come from his face with the back of one hand—and then was hauled to his feet and shoved against the door and kissed so hard and furious that he tasted blood. Before he could comment, or even really get his brain working again, Warren had his hose opened and was stroking him off quick and dirty, never letting up on the fierce kiss.

Bedros spilled into his hand after just a few minutes, feeding his moans and cries into Warren's greedy mouth, shuddering against him, grateful for the bracing offered by the door.

When he could more or less function again, he opened his eyes and swallowed, voice coming out slightly hoarse from the vigorous use it had just been given. "You certainly know how to give yourself a send-off."

Warren laughed, grabbed his shirt again, and dragged him across the room to the bed. "Shut up, Bedros."

Despite all the problems and other matters demanding Bedros's attention, he somehow wound up spending the entire rest of the afternoon and evening in his room with Warren. Most of it subject to Warren's every whim, until he was so wrung out he couldn't move.

Sleep had never come so quickly or easily, though he was chased by the depressing thought that this would be the one and only time his days ended so delightfully. If only he hadn't been so fucking stupid all those years ago.

He was stirred awake hours later by movement and chilly air slipping beneath the blankets, soft voices murmuring. Groaning, Bedros dragged himself out of bed to help, but mostly he just wound up standing around watching proceedings as he yawned so hard and often his eyes watered.

Though Warren, Nerek, and several others urged him to go back to bed, Bedros ignored them and headed downstairs and out of the great hall. He remained on the steps, hating the ache in his chest, the knots in his chest, as he watched the horses being brought out.

"Be careful," he said. "Both of you. Send word, Nerek, when you're on your way back. Wren, I'd appreciate you letting me know you're alive and well and back where you belong when this is over. After all we've come through, I'd hate for the bastards to get you now."

Warren left off where he'd been checking over his horse and climbed back up the steps. "No one is getting rid of me that easy. They tried, and thanks to you they failed. I'll let you know when I'm safe and home again." He stepped in, cupped Bedros's head, and kissed him thoroughly, leaving Bedros completely oblivious to the cold and more miserable than ever that this small slice of dream come true was leaving.

There was nothing he could say or do to convince Warren to come back. He had a whole life far, far south of Rehm, a life leagues better than snow and beer and absurdities like rainbow-colored chickens.

"I mean it," he said as they drew apart, fighting the urge, the need, to take another kiss. Why did kissing Warren feel a thousand times more right than every other kiss he'd had in his life? It made no sense, but there it was all the same. "Be careful. If they were willing to go to this much trouble, trying yet again to kill you isn't much of a stretch."

"We'll be careful, we'll be fine. Stop your fussing and go back to bed."

Bedros stepped back, every bit of him screaming to move in closer again. "Get going then, you soft southern noble. Nerek, good luck with your mother's estate and everything else. Don't take too long, or I'm sending Kohar to you."

Nerek laughed and swung up into the saddle. "That's not really a threat, you know."

"It will be when all his former customers recognize him," Bedros said.

Nerek glared, Kohar laughed, and with a wave and brief farewell, Warren led the way out of the yard.

Once they were out of sight, Bedros returned quietly to his room. His bed, which had always been a warm, safe haven, suddenly seemed a large, too big stretch of loneliness, a reminder of all that his past bad choices had cost him.

On that thrilling note, he fell back asleep, in no hurry to face the long, dreary day ahead of him.

*~*~*

It was three months before they received a letter from Nerek, and another two after that before they got a second one that promised he'd be home soon, or at least soon-ish.

When he did finally return home, it was in the dead of night while snow fell heavily down, a prelude to the final hoorah blizzard of the winter season.

"About time you got home," Bedros said, lifting a tankard of apple-berry ale in greeting. "Your lover has been positively wretched without you."

"He's wretched anyway," Nerek said with a smirk, eyes going past Bedros's shoulders to where Kohar had obviously appeared in the eastern entrance.

Bedros left them to it, more than happy to put his attention back on his ale and book, and leave hearing all about Nerek's trip until morning. He wasn't dead, he was home, and no army had shown up to punish them, so overall it seemed like a victory. The details could wait.

As Kohar finally let Nerek come up for air, though, they didn't hie off to his room. "Pardon, Your Grace…"

Dragging his eyes up slowly from his book, Bedros gave him a look. "Stop trying to butter me up and let's have it."

"I've a guest with me. Should be here in a moment. He got held up in the stables."

Bedros groaned. "Fine. Whatever. Go away. I'll have my revenge tomorrow, though."

Nerek smirked. "I doubt it."

On that mystifying note, he scooped up Kohar, who bellowed in outrage at being treated like a sack of vegetables but didn't actually seemed all that upset, and vanished from the great hall.

Sighing, Bedros climbed out of his delightfully warm cocoon and tried to make himself presentable. So much for a relaxing night for once. Nerek could have at least given him some details to work with, instead of leaving him utterly clueless about what sort of insane person would bother to come all the way out here during the last brutal, bitter gasp of winter before spring started to claw its way out in earnest.

He'd just set to work trying to tidy his hair by way of a hasty braid when the door crashed open, clearly snatched by the wind. A couple of guards went to deal with it, a battle they were long-used to, and the heavily cloaked figure who must be his guest hurried further into the hall and close to one of the small fires that were scattered about to keep the hall somewhat close to warm.

Before Bedros could ask, the guest flung back his hood—and Bedros forgot all about his hair, leaving it to unwind itself from the barely-begun braid as he stared in shock at Warren. "What are you doing here?"

Warren laughed, mouth curving into a smirk as it faded. "I'd think my husband would be happy to see me."

"That isn't funny," Bedros said, longing and hurt cutting through him, as sharp and awful as alcohol dumped on a fresh wound. "You're not. You never wanted to be. Under normal circumstances you'd never have agreed to even a ruse."

"Normal circumstances don't require a ruse." Warren's levity faded. "I… I admit I thought you'd be happy to see me. Should I go?"

"No!" Bedros said, and pressed his fists to his temples. "I'm mucking this up. Of course I'm happy to see you. I didn't think I'd see you again—ever. But I don't understand why you're here."

"Maybe we should continue this in your chambers?"

Bedros nodded and led the way, acutely, painfully aware of Warren the whole time. He smelled of sweat and earth and woodsmoke. Bedros wanted to strip him bare and push him into bed and stay there until the weather warmed or winter returned and it became impossible for Warren to leave again.

Instead, he closed the door and leaned against it, carefully not thinking of the last time he'd been up against it while Warren was in the room. "Is something else wrong? Were you not able to go home?"

Warren slowly removed his cloak and then stripped off his well-fitted gloves, tossing everything carelessly aside, eyes locked on Bedros the entire time. "I did return to my estate. Well, my former estate. I've been officially stripped of it, of everything, but I did so voluntarily. I had to return to attend paperwork and collect personal belongings and such, which should arrive here sometime in the spring, but all of that's attended now."

"I'm so sorry. You saved me, my people, my home, and it cost you literally everything."

Bedros could not remember a single moment in all the years they'd known each other that Warren had looked nervous, but right then he looked near to passing out. "Bedros, stop beating yourself up for things that aren't your fault, when you've clearly worked hard to make amends for the things that were your fault. Maybe you did His Majesty's bidding for too long, but you were also one of his earliest and greatest victims. You saved my life when you had absolutely no reason to do so, and every reason to let me die. I am here because I think we could be something, you and I, now that certain obstacles no longer keep us so far apart. I surrendered the place I called home because honestly, it hasn't felt like home in a long time. If you're willing, I'd like to see if Rehm could be the home I'm looking for. If… if you could be. If you'll stop punishing yourself and give us an honest try."

Another first: Bedros had never been much for crying, but right then his eyes stung quite a bit. "Are… are you serious? Why would you settle for me, Wren? You could have the whole world."

"I don't want the whole world. I want the man who calls me 'Wren' without thinking, when no one else in that stupid world I could supposedly have ever thought to give me a nickname." That smirk Bedros had always enjoyed a bit too much returned. "I admit I also like how… pliant you are. I liked having you under my thumb, Bedros."

"Your thumb? I'm pretty sure what you really want is me under your boot."

Oh, he *definitely* liked much how that made Warren's eyes *burn.*

He didn't even get to draw his next breath before he was pinned against the door again, wrists held firmly in place on either side of his head, Warren kissing him like it was the last thing he'd ever do. Bedros moaned and kissed him back, every crack and crevice of him that had appeared over the past months steadily filling.

When he eventually got a chance to speak again, all his clever remarks abandoned him. The only words he could manage were, "I missed you."

Warren smiled, soft and sweet, like nothing Bedros had ever seen but wanted to see at least ten thousand times more. "Does that mean I can stay?"

"You'd damn well better."

Laughing, Warren dragged him into another searing kiss and then dragged him off to their bed.

# THE MONK

The wind howled, high and whistling, accompanied by the cracking of ice and tree branches. They were sounds Taniel should have been long used to, given he'd dealt with them all his years in the monastery, but as ever, sleep would not come.

Sighing, he rolled out of bed and pulled on a heavy fur-trimmed robe before shuffling over to the fireplace. He settled in his chair, an old, threadbare thing left to be forgotten in a room used for storage. As a mage-in-residence, Taniel was entitled to his own room, something he'd never had before. He'd slept with his siblings as a child and youth, then with the other monks. He'd just assumed it would be the same here, but Bedros had issued him a room without even batting an eye.

Taniel certainly wasn't going to complain.

Though he had to admit it did get a little lonely sometimes. He liked people, being around them, interacting—being the center of attention. He really hadn't been a good monk at all, so it was for the best that chapter of his life was closed.

He missed the brotherhood of it, though. Castle Rehm was great, and home now, but he was still considered Kohar's brother before anything else. Just like always. Little brother. The adopted brother. The best part of the monastery was that he'd been seen as *him*, not the auxiliary of someone else.

Of course, Vosgi had preyed on that. Taniel cringed every time he thought about it, how quickly and easily he'd fallen for Vosgi, how certain he'd been they were the sort of love that would last a lifetime. He really should have known better. Nothing lasted a lifetime. Look at his family. One plague and they were gone. Another decade or two, nobody but him and Kohar would even remember them.

Argh, he hated when he couldn't sleep. All it did was turn him maudlin and whiny. Maybe he should just give up and get some work done.

Heaving a sigh, he threw back his cozy blanket and climbed to his feet, pulling his hair out of its loose sleep braid and braiding and wrapping it properly as he crossed the room to the portion of it dedicated to work, with a massive desk, racks of inks, bookshelves, a worktable for making his inks and other things, and far more besides. It was as fine as the workrooms he'd shared back at the monastery, and even better because he didn't have to share it.

He'd only just sat down and lit his lamps, though, when a knock came at his door. Who in the world would be knocking on his door at… He glanced at a nearby clock. Half past two in the morning. Taniel went to open it and stared a moment in surprise.

Lieutenant Corsair. Handsome. Dashing. Elegant and refined. A deeply admired and adored local, and Nerek's protégé. Taniel would love to do any number of things to him, from sweet to 'how does a monk know how to do that.' But he wasn't going to mess up this latest chance at having a home, building a life, by adding stupid things like sex and romance to the pile. He'd learned his lesson with Vosgi, who was really just the last and greatest mistake in a long string of attempts at One True Love.

Some people were made for such things. Like

Kohar. Others weren't. It was long past time Taniel accepted he was one of those.

Still, a small part of him couldn't help but hope that Corsair had shown up in the dark of night offering to help him sleep.

"I'm sorry to bother you," Corsair said, immediately dashing that tiny, feeble hope, "but I may have a problem in the village. I saw some strange marks while on patrol. I was deliberating on whether to wake you or Kohar when I saw you moving around. I don't suppose you'd come tell me if it's something to worry about?"

"Of course. Let me get dressed. Come on in, this hallway is miserably cold."

"Thanks." Corsair stepped into the room and closed the door as Taniel went to get dressed, heading over to the fireplace and immediately stripping off his gloves to better warm his hands. He looked good bathed in firelight, but also tired and wrung out.

Unlike Taniel, who looked sickly pale all the time thanks to white skin and a place that spent most of the year buried in snow. Corsair had warm brown skin with yellow undertones and curly brown hair with just the faintest hint of red to it. His eyes were a dark amber, though they warmed and brightened when he was happy or amused. Taniel would love to know what they looked like when—

Nope. Cutting that thought off right there.

He discarded his soft, warm robe and shivered as he hastily pulled clothes from his wardrobe and yanked them on. Hose, tunic, a winter robe that fastened versus the summer style that was meant to drape open, and fur-lined boots and fur-trimmed cloak. He grabbed the satchel that held the tools and spells he needed for most problems, and finally joined Corsair by the fire. "All set."

"My horse is waiting, if you don't mind riding with me, though I can wake the stable hands to get you a horse of your own if you prefer."

"I can ride yo—with you," Taniel replied, hoping desperately Corsair hadn't noticed his stupid slip.

Outside, it was even more miserable than the drafty castle, the wind so sharp that breathing hurt. Corsair swung up easily into the saddle, then offered a hand to help Taniel up, and a moment later they were off, riding steadily but carefully through the dark night and endless drifts of snow. The frequent traffic between castle and village had worn a path through the mess, but that did nothing to lessen the danger of ice, especially the kind that wasn't even visible.

They traveled in silence, Corsair's attention taken up wholly by the treacherous going. All around them the wind made the trees crackle and crunch, and every now and then he could hear an owl's cry, the rustle of nocturnal animals foraging through the snowy underbrush for whatever meals they could find.

High above, the stars glittered wherever the clouds broke up enough to see them. To judge by the clouds, though, there'd be more snow come morning, and there was no such thing as a light dusting at Castle Rehm. Spring was theoretically close, but winter always went out with a bitter fight.

Everything was dark and quiet when they arrived. There were a few lamps lit, at the healer's house and the outpost the guards worked from when assigned a village rotation. Otherwise, there was only limited moonlight to see by and the torch that Corsair lit once he'd dismounted. "This way." He patted the horse and then crunched off through the snow, following a path less tramped out than the one they'd taken into the village.

They went past a couple of homes, then around and behind one to a large shed behind it, the kind used for storing foodstuffs and other supplies for winter.

Behind it, drawn onto the back wall, were marks that made Taniel's blood run colder than anything the frigid weather could do. Please let him be wrong. "Bring that torch closer. I need to see it as clearly as possible." He strode across the cracking snow and dropped to his knees, close enough to examine the mark but carefully not touching it. Corsair came up behind him and held the torch so it cast a perfect amount of light across the spell.

Taniel swore.

"That bad?"

"Worse," Taniel said grimly, pulling his satchel from his shoulders. First he yanked out the case that held his special rune spectacles and slid them into place. They were a fancier version of his brother's costly rune monocle, allowing him to see magic at a level of detail that had given him a headache for months until he'd grown accustomed. Writing spells was hard enough, but when ancient, forbidden magic was brought into the picture… a monocle wasn't enough. His glasses had two different lenses—the standard rune glass used in monocles on the left side; the right lens was darker, meant to see special inks and spells that the first lens wasn't powerful enough to. Combined, there was very little the spectacles could not see.

Only twenty monks, out of hundreds, had ever been approved and fitted for rune spectacles. When he'd been cast out, they'd wanted to destroy his, but they belonged rightfully and wholly to Taniel, and he hadn't been banned from magic, just from the monastery and their collection of esoteric magic.

Right now, Taniel almost wished he wasn't one of those twenty, because seeing the spell in full detail only drove home how horrific it was. Drawing out paper and pen next, he sketched out the spell as best he could and filled two more pages with notes and theories, heedless of the snow rapidly freezing him to death.

"Can you destroy it?" Corsair asked when he paused. "Whatever it is, clearly it needs to go."

"It's a demon summon, way worse than the succubus he used before. That was child's play compared to this. Worse, this is just one part. If I'm right, there are six more of these around the village, or will be soon. I don't know how far he's gotten." Taniel chewed on his thumbnail. "Making just one would take several hours. A bare minimum of five, and honestly it should be closer to eight."

"There's no way we would have missed him on our patrols. We've been beyond diligent ever since the royal army attacked, and before that because of the succubus. Captain has had us on constant, overlapping shifts. We would have noticed a strange figure in the village."

"Not if he was using magic to make sure he went unnoticed," Taniel replied, anger and fear churning in his stomach. "It's dangerous, costly magic, but well within Vosgi's range."

"So you do think it's him?"

"Who else would it be? I just wish he'd find something better to do with his time. I never should have come here; it's just encouraging him to keep hurting everyone here."

"If he wasn't hurting and killing us, he'd be hurting and killing elsewhere. There's nothing you can do about that, so don't blame yourself."

Taniel nodded, somewhat comforted that Corsair was trying to help, even if the words themselves did nothing. It *was* his fault. He'd fancied himself in love, and he'd used that love to justify letting things get too far. By the time he'd spoken up, it was too late—and turning Vosgi in had just compounded the problem, adding anger and a vindictive need for revenge on top of Vosgi's obsession with magic and power.

He stood, putting his papers and pen away, and removing the glasses, tucking them into his hair atop his head. He was exhausted already, and the work hadn't even begun.

"So you can't destroy it or whatever?"

"I can, but not right now. I only brought my basics along, thinking we'd missed something done by royal soldiers or spies. I wasn't expecting one seventh of a summoning spell for a class four demon."

Corsair stared at him blankly. "Class four is obviously bad, but I'm not familiar. How bad are we talking?"

"The concubus he summoned last year was a class one. Summoning a demon at all, without piles upon piles of permission and enough paperwork to fill the castle, results in being barred from using magic and usually a long, if not lifelong, prison sentence. Anything above a class two is grounds for execution, often immediate." Taniel shook his head. " ven for Vosgi, a class four seems far too dangerous and risky. I don't know what the hells he's thinking, doing something this… this… frankly 'fucking stupid' doesn't begin to do it justice. This is beyond comprehension."

"We'd better get back and inform the others."

"Go ahead. I'm going to stay and look for the other parts of the spell. Kohar will know what to bring me."

"I'm not leaving you alone out here, not with that utter bastard roaming around."

Taniel snorted. "I'm the safest person in Rehm,

Lieutenant. He won't kill me until I've suffered enough for my betrayal. Until he feels I have finally been adequately punished. Go get the others—and be careful. You're in far more danger than me."

"Fine, but have a care, all right?"

"I will. Trust me, I learned my lesson a long time ago."

Corsair thrust the torch into a pile of hardened snow and with a last admonishing look, strode off.

After he'd ridden off, and Taniel could no longer hear any hint of him, he reached into his satchel and withdrew a bottle of ink and a long, thin wooden box. Inside was a special pen for writing magic, the tip made of bone. Human bone, freely donated by a monk before he'd passed away, but edging close to illegal all the same. With the pen easy to access, he removed his gloves, drew the knife on his belt, and slit his left palm, cupping his hand so it pooled. Into the blood he carefully added a few small drops of ink, mixing it with the tip of the pen before drawing enough to write with.

He started at the top, the north point, and worked slowly down and around in a circle slightly larger than the demon summon. When he reached the bottom, he returned to the top and worked his way back down, until the eastern and western halves joined up at the south point.

By the time he finished, he was exhausted, and his hand was not remotely happy with him. Grimacing, he cleaned it off as best he could with snow and a clean kerchief, then wrapped it in a temporary bandage he'd be able to easily remove later before putting his gloves back on.

Tucking away the rest of his supplies, save the pen, he crouched one more time and drew the final, activating rune. The spell came to life with a lurid red shine and settled into a dull, dying-embers glow.

Now he just had to find and cage the rest of them. That wouldn't stop Vosgi, but it would slow the bastard down as he wouldn't be able to break the binding without fresh blood from Taniel. He really hoped Vosgi took that option, and their inevitable reunion came that much sooner—but he wasn't holding his breath. Vosgi was clever and skilled and ruthless, and that last one was the deadliest. There was very little magic couldn't do, or help with, when the mage wasn't held back by things like 'murder is wrong.'

Reaching into his bag again, he retrieved his sketchbook and flipped to a rough sketch of the village he'd done a few weeks ago. One of several, actually, as sketches of his surroundings always proved to be damned useful, especially regarding magic. He marked off the first circle they'd found, though if he was correct, it was actually the fourth in the set of seven.

With that marked, it was simple enough to make educated guesses at a couple of potential spots for the next mark, and once he had two marked, the rest would come easy.

If only getting rid of Vosgi was as easy as locking up his work.

Taniel walked as quickly as he could, eager to find as many of the summon circles as possible before Corsair returned with an extremely irate Kohar, who would know damn good and well there was no way to simply destroy a summon like this. Level four demons were illegal in part because they required a maximum blood sacrifice—the life of a living creature, a large one, like a wolf or deer. Or human.

Destroying them was far more difficult and costly than that. Demons were easy to summon, near impossible to be rid of, at least at level three and beyond. All things considered, they'd gotten off pretty lightly with the concubus.

If he didn't get to Vosgi in time, they wouldn't be so lucky this time around. Especially since he still didn't know what kind of demon exactly Vosgi had chosen. That it was a class four narrowed the possibilities some, but still left entirely too many options, and one spell circle wasn't enough to settle the matter. He'd need to see at least four of the seven, if not more.

He'd just found the second circle, tucked away behind some old barrels and crates behind the baker's shop, when the snap and crackle of the night was drowned out by a furious bellow. "Tani! Get your ass out here right fucking now!"

Groaning, putting away the knife he'd just drawn to reopen the wound in his hand, Taniel heaved back to his feet and went to go deal with his brother.

He'd only just reached the street when Kohar spotted him. "You!"

"Me," Taniel said. "What are you yelling about?"

"What are you doing mucking about with demons all alone! You're smarter than this!"

Taniel gave him a withering look. "Yes, I am, and the very last thing I want is innocent people dead if something goes wrong. Anyway, I was fine, exactly as I knew it would be."

Corsair looked at him with an expression so frosty the snow around them was warm by comparison. "So you just sent me after Kohar to get me out of the way?"

"It wasn't like that," Taniel said. "I really do need stuff that only Kohar could bring me. I also wanted to get started on solving this problem. It's grisly, dangerous work, and the fewer people around, the better. So thanks, Kohar, for waking up the entire damned village with your melodramatic screaming."

Kohar narrowed his eyes in a way that did not bode well for Taniel's continued existence. Fortunately, or unfortunately, Taniel was long used to that look. Nobody was less impressed with a person than their siblings.

"Great, now that everybody is pissed off with me, did you bring what I need?" Taniel asked. "Yelling at me can wait. Demons cannot."

"You'll be lucky if yelling is all I do," Kohar replied, even as he swung his satchel off his shoulder and set it on a nearby barrel. "Does the monastery know you have some of those books in your room?"

Taniel groaned. "Oh, my gods you're worse than Mom ever was." He snatched the book Kohar held out and flipped through it, looking for anything that matched what he'd so far seen. "I didn't steal anything, fuck you. All those copies were *mine.* I paid for the supplies; I paid the monastery for the time *I* spent copying them. Good to know your high opinion of me." He started to turn yet another page, then stopped. "Bring that torch closer."

Corsair did so, and Taniel swore. "Come on, I need to take a look at two circles I've found so far." He strode off back to the second one, barely noticing as Corsair and Kohar followed him.

It was, unfortunately, right where he'd left it. As they drew close, Kohar pulled out his monocle and affixed it in place. "I've never actually come across a spell so complicated parts of it were hidden from me."

Taniel didn't reply, too focused on the circle and his book. He drew a pencil from his bag and ripped a page from his sketchbook. Sitting down, heedless of the snow that quickly sank through his layers, he drew out the circle in front of him. When he was done, it exactly matched the one right below where he'd been drawing. He could have traced it, even though he hadn't. "Fuck."

He stood and raced off back to the first circle, ignoring the swearing and cursing behind him, and repeated the whole thing there.

With the same grim results.

Kohar snatched the book out of his hand, scowling at the circles he'd drawn, comparing them to the page they matched with. "This is way beyond me. It's a demon, I can tell that much, but only that much."

"It doesn't say?" Corsair asked.

"No," Kohar and Taniel said together, and Taniel added, "It's to mitigate people doing stupid shit like this. We learn and memorize the various runes and other markings, and they can only be cast with the special inks I have, inks that even someone of Kohar's skill couldn't easily make or obtain. Normally the system works well, but there's always…" He sighed. "There's always dumbasses like me and Vosgi around, who know far too much and yet somehow still not enough. I still need to see the other circles, as the two so far aren't enough to narrow the demon down precisely, but they're already pointing toward violence. Destruction, blood, something like that."

Corsair's eyes widened. "What in the world does a demon of blood do?"

"Drink it," Taniel said grimly. "Until there's not a single drop left in the whole village. Every kill makes it stronger, increasingly difficult to stop. Turns its victims into walking corpses that devour the living."

"That sounds…" Corsair didn't finish, but he looked dangerously close to screaming or puking or both.

Taniel turned away. "I need to cage the second circle, and then we need to find the rest."

"You're *caging* them? Damn it, Tani, I'm going to—"

"To what?" Taniel asked, half-turning to face

him. "Stop me? You can't, and we both know it. That aside, what other choice do I have? I can't just throw together the kind of sacrifice necessary to break this kind of spell. All I can do right now is slow him down and hopefully force him into the open, so I can put the bastard down once and for all. If you have a better idea, by all means say, but until then, let me do the only thing I'm good for."

He stormed off back through the tracks they'd made in the snow to the second circle. Pulling out his tools, he re-opened the wound in his hand and set to work.

By the time he was done, he was ready to go back to bed and stay there, but he was only two down, five to go. He was frozen clear through to the bone, probably from sitting in the snow like a dumbass, but that was also a problem for later.

He trudged onward, hand aching, head hurting, exhausted and cold and sick at heart, looking carefully until he found the third circle. His head felt like it was being stabbed repeatedly by the time he was done with that one.

"Are you all right?" Corsair asked.

"Fine," Taniel said. "I'm going to need some sleep when I'm done, but I'm fine."

Kohar muttered, but thankfully didn't press the matter, though he must know the severity of what Taniel was doing. There wasn't anyone else to do it, though. For better or worse, Taniel knew—and was damned good at—arcane magic. The more forbidden, the better. He genuinely loved it. He'd stupidly thought Vosgi loved it too. Loved him.

Vosgi, however, just loved the power and violence. Loved the way it made people afraid of him.

Taniel he'd never cared about at all. Not until his faithful, gullible lackey had betrayed him, anyway.

Thankfully, with three circles down, the remaining four were increasingly easy to find, though each one was exhausting in its own right to cage, and his poor hand felt like it was on fire. He'd be lucky if he was able to use it at all in the next week, if not two. Normally he'd take it from his arm, fill a bowl, but walking around in the snow it was easier to just slit his hand and use that as an improvised bowl.

Well, nothing healing spells and rest wouldn't fix eventually. It was the least he deserved, really.

By the time he finally finished caging all seven circles, sealing away the summon until Vosgi managed to kidnap him, or whatever he did, Taniel's vision was swimming. He sat down in the snow again, barely noticing Kohar yelling at him. From there, it seemed so easy, and like such a good idea, to just go ahead and lie down. The snow was so cool, and he was so hot…

He woke to a dire need to piss and a stomach growling for food. The first matter was easily addressed, at least after he unearthed himself from what seemed to be roughly five hundred blankets. Who was trying to smother him with blankets?

Well, that was a stupid question. His worrywart brother of course. He really was as bad as their mother had been. Funny that Taniel hadn't noticed until now.

Once he'd pissed, cleaned up, and dressed, he went in search of food.

Instead, he found Corsair, sitting right outside his door reading a book and sipping tea. He looked up at the same time Taniel asked, "What in the world are you doing there?"

"Kohar wanted you watched," Corsair replied. "I volunteered. He wanted me inside your room, but that seemed unnecessary. Too high up to go through the window, especially with everything iced over."

Taniel sighed. "Everyone's faith in me is truly astounding. How long have I been asleep?"

"Not quite twelve hours. How's your hand?"

"Oh, uh…" Taniel looked down at it, but Kohar had clearly done impeccable work as usual, because there was nothing left but a scar. "It's fine. Better than it should be, really, but Kohar knows what he's doing."

Corsair closed his book and rose. "My impression so far is that as good as he is, you leave him well behind."

Taniel froze, stared in surprise. It was true, no ego or delusions required, but growing up no one had really acknowledged that he was at least as promising a mage as Kohar. He'd just been the little brother—the little orphan boy—copying Kohar. Even though he loved magic wholly in his own right. He'd never needed anyone to give him his love of magic. Kohar had just happened to love the same thing, and he was older, and not a sad little orphan, and so it must be that Taniel was copying him.

"It's not a contest," he finally said. "It's true I study things more esoteric and dangerous, things I'm lucky not to have been arrested for. I've said that a hundred times already, though. Can I go in search of food, or does my brother think he's grounded me?"

"If your brother wanted you to stay in your room, I'm pretty sure manacles and curses would be involved."

Taniel rolled his eyes because that was true. "Come on, then, we'll get me food and you your freedom. I'm sorry you've been stuck in this hallway while I slept."

"Like I said, I volunteered," Corsair replied. "It beats being stuck out in the snow on patrol or breaking up drunks or finding the drunks who wandered into the woods." He sighed. "I was gone nearly ten years, and when I finally came back, this place hadn't changed at all. It's comforting and confounding all at once."

Corsair had never said so much to him, just him, since Taniel's arrival. He tried not to assume that meant something, especially since the last time they'd spoken Corsair had been angry with him. "That sounds nice, honestly. I traveled back to the city a couple of times while still with the monastery, and it wasn't the same at all. I don't think I could ever live there again, not after… everything."

"What do you mean?" Corsair asked with a frown.

Taniel stopped abruptly, staring at him in surprise. "Did Kohar never say?"

"He honestly doesn't talk much about himself, not really, except maybe to Nerek."

"I see," Taniel said with a sigh, because that did sound like Kohar. "Our family—immediate, extended, all of them—died in the plague, minus a couple who'd died before the plague struck. We were the only two left, other than a smattering of very distant relatives we didn't really associate with. He came here. I went to the monastery."

"Gods above," Corsair said, and then stunned Taniel a second time by abruptly stepping in and hugging him tightly. "I'm so sorry. I don't know what I'd do if such a thing happened to me. You have my deepest sympathies."

"Th-thank you," Taniel replied, hugging him back tentatively. It wasn't something people really did with him anymore. His family had been extremely tactile, but Kohar had become less so since that horrible fucking time. Then he stepped back and cleared his throat. "I didn't mean to turn the conversation so depressing. I should have guessed Kohar would be all hush hush. That's how he is, for all that he can run his mouth endlessly."

Corsair laughed. "I would never dare suggest or even hint at such a thing about Mage-in-Residence Kohar. Unless he wasn't actually in residence at the moment."

Taniel's laughter joined Corsair's as they resumed walking, bound for the great hall, the smell of food getting ever stronger. Roast duck, by the scent, and the skin would be all crispy and covered in herbs and butter with a blood sauce to accompany, a thick chowder with vegetables and chicken… the dark, nutty bread he loved so much, with butter and jams and more to accompany it. Pies made from dinner leftovers, stuffed with boar and venison and thick gravy, cheese, roasted pumpkin and squash, dried fruit soaked in liquor, beer and mead and wine…

If there was one thing he'd missed about life beyond the monastery, it was the variety of food. The monastery food was good, but it was limited and on a strict, unbending schedule. The castle had something of a schedule, but mostly worked with what was available each day.

As ever, the hall was bustling, people coming and going as they went about their chores and errands for the day. In one corner several women worked on sewing, from simple repairs to elaborate embroidery. There were people cleaning the floor, replacing rushes where necessary, others dealing with the dirty dishes or bringing in fresh platters and bowls of food.

In the center of it all, dealing with various the problems brought to him, was Warren, which meant Bedros must be out riding the perimeter today, or putting out a proverbial fire somewhere. Bedros had been the duke of the castle for several years now, but

Warren had arrived only recently—first to save the castle and village from being slaughtered, and then to remain permanently. Whatever complicated history he and Bedros had, they'd put it behind them for a happier future.

Why couldn't Vosgi have chosen him over magic? But that presumed Vosgi had ever considered him a choice, rather than a means to an end and the occasional bedwarmer. Gods, every time he thought about it, he just felt stupider and more depressed.

Shoving the miserable thoughts away, he double checked the hall for Kohar and then, when the coast seemed clear, headed straight for the table where the food was laid out and loaded as much as he could onto two plates. Setting them at the nearest available seat, he went to fetch a cup and then sat down, filling the cup with beer from a nearby pitcher, one of several scattered across each table, and then tucked in.

Corsair sat down across from him with a slightly smaller amount of food, chuckling as he poured himself a cup of mulled wine. "Everyone makes jokes about how much soldiers eat, but I swear mages leave us in the cold."

Taniel laughed. "I won't argue. I assume, since you haven't brought it up, that my cages are still working and nothing else has happened in the past twelve hours?"

"If it has, no one has told me," Corsair replied, and paused to take a large bite of roasted duck. "Kohar has been in the village keeping an eye on things, and Nerek has sent out additional patrols. He's riding perimeter with Bedros, I believe. I saw them leave a couple of hours ago. Sadly, I don't see why searching will produce anything this time when it's never worked before, but even Kohar doesn't know how to find this slimy bastard trying to murder us all." He forked up more duck and a few bites of carrot and squash. "You never did get a chance to say what kind of demon we're dealing with. Kohar thinks that blood demon thing you mentioned, but he wasn't sure."

"He's right," Taniel said quietly. He'd been desperately avoiding thinking about it since waking up, focusing only on immediate needs, but as his stomach settled down, it was hard to ignore the enormous problem hanging over their heads. Vosgi was trying to summon a demon of blood, one of the nastiest, meanest types, and nearly impossible to kill or banish. "Do you know when everyone will be back?"

"Probably not until around sunset, if not after."

Taniel nodded. "That'll give me time to compile more information. Thankfully, with the cages successfully cast, Vosgi's only choices are to find me to break them or start over completely with his summon circles. Which is not really viable, not with all the time and energy and blood he's already invested."

"Why would he need you to break the cages?"

"It's my blood that made them, and so it's only my blood that can break them. The one benefit of being an orphan is that no one can use Kohar's blood instead. There's only me."

"I see," Corsair said quietly. "It sounds like you've had a horrible life."

"No, no." Taniel set his spoon down. "I wouldn't want anyone to think that. My birth parents, whoever the hells they were, threw me out to die on the street. I was taken in by a big, warm, loving family. I got to live, and got to shape that life, with nothing forced upon me. I lost that family, yes. I doubt Kohar and I will ever entirely recover, no matter how much we've learned to cope in the day to day. We didn't even get to put them on pyres; they were just thrown into a mass grave." He shook his head before the memories got the better of him. "I got to study the kind of magic I always wanted, *master* the kind of magic I always wanted. That came with problems too, but I brought those problems on myself. I'm very fortunate with the life I've led. Everybody hits rough moments—some small, some large. I just wish the problem of my ex-lover had not spread to this entire damned village." He picked up his spoon and stabbed at a piece of potato in his bowl of chowder. "I've forced his hand now, though, the infuriating bastard. He'll have to come for me if he wants his precious demon, and when he does, I'll take care of him once and for all."

When they'd finished eating and had dropped off their dishes, he fixed a large mug of tea and took it with him as he headed off back to his room—with Corsair still at his side. "You don't have to keep watching me. I'm not going to do anything untoward."

"I don't believe you," Corsair replied. "One, just because you have no plans right now doesn't mean that won't become an option later. Two, I'm under orders to watch you until further notice."

"Fine, fine," Taniel replied. If only Corsair was tagging along because he wanted to spend time with Taniel. Whatever. He had more important matters to deal with right now. "You've been warned, though. Have fun not nodding off while I read through a stack of dry, dusty tomes."

Corsair chuckled. "Try standing night watch in the dead of winter."

"Try sitting through it chanting the whole time," Taniel replied with a grin.

That got him an actual laugh. "All right, monk. Fair enough. Why do you have to sit around chanting all night?"

"I actually liked that part. It had a lot of purposes. Discipline, focus, becoming closer to your brothers and the gods… It's also just plain beautiful. One of the few things I miss."

"It does sound beautiful, the few times I've heard you doing it, in the castle's temple and when you climb to the roof."

Taniel hoped the dim-lit halls hid his flush. "I didn't realize I'd drawn attention."

"We don't really have a lot of monks lying around the place," Corsair said with one of his adorable crooked smiles. "Just a priest who worships wine and beer and cider as much as the rest of the village." He opened the door to Taniel's room as they reached it and bowed slightly as Taniel walked by him.

"Quit that," Taniel said, flustered for no good reason.

Corsair just gave a sly little grin and followed him inside, taking a seat at the table in the corner where Taniel had arranged a mini library for his hard-won collection of twenty-three books. They'd had to travel behind him, along with the rest of his meager belongings, minus the two he simply hadn't been willing to trust to the haulers he'd hired.

Setting down his mug, Taniel went to the shelves and pulled down the books he needed. "So how did you come to be named Corsair?"

Sighing long and loud, Corsair replied, "My mother loves fanciful tales, and her favorites were those about pirates. The ones she heard, though, were told by a man who thought 'corsair' was a name, not a term, and she was my mother's favorite pirate in those tales, so that's my name."

Taniel laughed. "That's utterly charming."

"Not always," Corsair muttered. "My whole time through training and assignment in the city, I was only ever called 'Pirate.' It got old fast."

Taniel just laughed some more. "Oh, gods, I can

imagine the jokes. Did you shiver many timbers, Lieutenant? Plunder many a chest? Dive—"

"Stop it! Stop it!" Corsair said, torn between laughing and groaning, covering his face with his hands. "You're as bad as the rest of them."

"I was the youngest of quite the hoard, I'm *worse* than most." Sitting down, Taniel sipped at his tea before sliding on his spectacles as he opened the first of his books, his levity falling by the wayside as he plunged into studies of demons.

Someone, likely Kohar, had left his notes on the table and hung his satchel on its hook. Taniel pulled out the drawings of the circles he'd done, studying them intently as he compared them to the charts in his book. Having full light to work by, instead of battling snow and wind while working by lantern light, it was even more painfully apparent what they were dealing with.

"A demon of blood for certain," he said. "If Vosgi summons him successfully… this village won't survive, and neither will any of the surrounding, because the only people who could stop a demon like this are weeks, if not months, away. They'd arrive too fucking late."

"You caged the summon, though, right?"

"Yes. As long as Vosgi doesn't get me before I get him, all will be well."

"What should we do if he *does* get you."

"Kill him if you can. If you can't, kill me. Dead blood is useless."

Corsair frowned—glowered, really. "No, fuck that. I'm not killing you. Have you lost your gods-damned mind?"

"No, I haven't," Taniel said flatly. "I know Vosgi better than anyone, all that he is capable of and will gladly do. You don't *understand.* This demon will be invisible. Intangible. It will sneak into homes like a breeze or a shadow. It will sink its fangs into the neck of its victim and drain every drop of blood from their body. The person will seem dead. Until a few hours later ,when they rise and walk again, a rotting shell of what they once were, with an insatiable craving for the flesh of the living. The numbers of dead-walkers will grow and grow, spreading out like a plague, passing it on to anyone they attack that doesn't become a meal. By the time help arrives, there will be nothing left, save thousands upon thousands of monsters that were once people, who will have to be eradicated like vermin, and there will never be *any* guarantee they got them all."

Corsair's skin had lost all its color.

"I am all that is keeping that from happening right now," Taniel continued. "So yes, if the choice is kill me or let a demon commit mass murder, then there isn't really much of a choice at all."

"Your brother…"

"Would never forgive me, but he'd also understand," Taniel said with a sigh. "Hopefully it won't come to that. My plan is to kill Vosgi. I'm only giving you the last resort."

"It's been noted," Corsair said. "Now tell me what I hope to gods is a far more effective and less depressing plan."

Taniel spread his hands. "I wish I could give you one, but if it was possible to find Vosgi, we'd have done so by now. All I can do is wait for him to come after me. In the meantime, I am learning all I can about the demon itself, the requirements to banish it, and practicing every nasty trick I can think of to deal with Vosgi."

Corsair hesitated, then asked, "It is true you two were… close? I've heard your offhand comments, bits of conversation, but it's hard to believe you'd… tolerate someone like Vosgi, let alone be…"

"His lover?" Taniel laughed sourly. "Vosgi didn't start out a monster. At least, he didn't seem like one for a long time. Maybe he just hid it well, or maybe I was blind. Probably I was blind. Anyway, he was always cocky, reckless… but he was, is, smart, beautiful, and captivating. He seemed to know every last one of my weak points, and he exploited them ruthlessly. I didn't see it at first, and then I resisted seeing it… and then it was too late. I turned us in, and now we're here. I thought he loved me, but all he wanted was a biddable assistant."

"I know the type," Corsair said quietly. "Met several of them in the army. Most often they were brass. What could a cretin like that ever offer you, though?"

Taniel shook his head. The shame, the humiliation, the stupid happiness he'd believed was real for far too long, burned through them, roiled in his stomach like spoiled food. "It doesn't matter. Stupid, foolish things. I should have realized he never saw me as anything but an easy target."

"That's not how it works. I've seen it more times than I care to count. The only one to blame for any of this is Vosgi. We'll get the bastard. I'm sorry he used you. No one should ever be treated that way."

"No, but I'm not innocent either. I enjoyed the thrill of learning forbidden magic as much as he did. I just never wanted to hurt anyone. It doesn't matter. Whining doesn't solve problems."

"Wounds need lancing before they can heal, though."

Taniel smiled weakly and went back to his reading, not really certain what to say. Really he just wanted to crawl into bed and smother himself with a pillow. Anything but sit there tolerating Corsair's pity. He was *tired* of pity.

The books, sadly, couldn't tell him much that he didn't already know. What it could tell him, however, was useful: when the demon was best summoned and how to banish it.

Banishing was useless. Demons of this level required exactly the blood sacrifice he'd feared: a human being. He'd thought something like a deer or other large animal would work, but he'd been wrong.

Of far more interest was the summoning time: three days from now, when the sky was moonless and the stars were in the 'winter diamond' alignment.

The knowledge brought a troubling realization, of course.

"What's wrong? Corsair asked. "You look like you've… well, seen a demon."

"This type of demon is best cast under very particular conditions. Those conditions happen in three days, and they only occur once every ten years. Either Vosgi has been planning this for a very long time, or he saw a chance when he was deciding what demon to summon. If it's the first…"

"There's no telling what he's really up to, what else he's already done," Corsair finished. "Mercy of the gods, this man is terrifying. Every time I think he can't possibly get worse, he proves me horrifically wrong."

Taniel flinched. His fault. This was all his fault. He'd supported a monster and then betrayed him, and made Vosgi a thousand times worse than he might have otherwise been. At the very least, he'd sped up the process. Gods, if only he hadn't been so fucking weak and gullible.

"Hey." It was the soft touch to his hand, more than the gentle tone, that drew Taniel's gaze up. "It's not your fault. I know that's hard to believe, no matter how many times you hear it, but Vosgi is the only one responsible for his actions. He chose to do illegal things; he chose to lash out when you did the right thing. He chose to come here and murder people. Nobody else. If it hadn't been you to piss him off, it would have been someone or something else. He was always looking for an excuse. Trust me, I can tell you about several officers with the same damn tendencies. They walked in every day looking, damn near begging for a reason to punish someone. They're impossible to deal with, and they excel especially at making everyone around them feel bad, feel like they deserve the abuse. Don't let him get to you."

Taniel smiled. "Thank you. You're right: it's hard to believe. I'll always feel horrible about the way I helped him, and that it was my decision, my actions, that drove him *here* to enact his terrible plans. But I'll try."

"Good. So are there any other conditions that need to be met to summon the demon? Something we can prevent, destroy, whatever?"

Taniel pursed his lips as he read over the notes again. Much like the summon circles themselves, the book was careful never to plainly state which notes referred to which demons, but someone with the proper knowledge would have no trouble puzzling out the encrypted identifiers at the head of each section. "Not really. He's already drawn the circles in the most ideal arrangement. He's doing it on blood-soaked ground. No wonder he was helping the royal army." He sighed. "I don't think circumstances could have come together any better for him if he'd tried. Everything from the weather to the recent fighting to the stars is perfect for him."

"So you're really not kidding when you say that all that stands between success and failure is him kidnapping you."

"I'm really not."

"Then we have to find a way to protect you."

"You have to find an effective way to use me as bait," Taniel replied.

Corsair's mouth pinched. "Even if I was willing to go that route, which I'm not, there's no way Kohar would ever permit it."

"Kohar isn't the boss of me, whatever he and everyone else thinks," Taniel snapped. "I'm not a pathetic little orphan boy anymore. I knew what I was doing when I caged those circles. This was never going to end any way except with me facing Vosgi. Nor does it matter what you're 'willing' to do. The simple fact is that he has no choice but to come for me. It's going to happen, no matter what any of us wants or doesn't want. We may as well use that fact against him."

Brows rising sharply, Corsair said, "I thought you and Kohar were close. Why does it always sound like you resent him?"

Taniel turned away, sighing and dragging a hand through his hair. "I don't resent him. I resent I'm never seen as anything but the pitiful little orphan thrown out like so much garbage and lucky to be taken in by such a perfect family, and isn't it cute how he copies Kohar's interest in magic?"

"Ah," Corsair said. "My youngest sister feels that way often, or at least similarly, since she was never an orphan. I am sorry. I'm the eldest, so it's not exactly a problem I can commiserate with, but I know how much it hurts her to always feels like she's in the shadow of the rest of us. It's been better since she got engaged and spends more time out on her betrothed's farm. He was one of the injured in the fight against the royal army, but thankfully a few more weeks rest and he'll be fine."

"That's good to hear," Taniel said. "I hate so many people were killed and wounded, and it's why I'm not going to let anyone tell me I can't do this. I'm the only one who can, and I will."

Corsair sighed, head falling back briefly before he lifted it again and said, "All right, then. I'll help as best I can. But I don't like it, and I reserve the right to alter whatever crazy plan we come up with should a better solution present itself."

"Fair enough."

"So do you have a plan yet?"

"Vosgi is going to snatch me, that's a fact. What we need is a way to track *me* that he won't be able to find and destroy, since that's the first thing he'll look for. But every magic trick I know, he knows how to break."

"Mages," Corsair said with a laugh. His chair scraped the floor as he pushed away from the table and stood. Circling around, he reached up around his neck and undid what proved to be a leather cord with metal clasps. "Up."

Taniel obeyed, unable to not notice how nice Corsair smelled, like sweat and smoke and leather, the beautiful hints of red in his dark hair, how badly he wanted to twine his fingers through those springy curls. If only, if only.

It was only when Corsair finished fastening the necklace around Taniel's neck and stepped back that Taniel could breathe properly again, though he'd gladly give up breathing to keep Corsair close just a few minutes more. Ah, well.

He focused on the necklace, which proved to be a tiny glass vial with a cork stopper, filled with a gleaming oil that smelled of cinnamon, cloves, and other things he couldn't name. "What is this?"

"A finder, we call them," Corsair said. "It's a local thing. Every family has hunting dogs trained to follow the unique scents of their family. Any outsiders ask, we call them perfumers, since it doesn't hurt they smell nice, after all. You don't always need magic, mage-in-residence, to solve a problem. I doubt Vosgi will pay it any mind, if he notices at all."

Taniel smiled, excitement running through as an idea caught fire. "Especially if we *do* use some magical means. He'll find them all, break them, and be so smugly pleased with himself he definitely won't pay attention to a silly little vial of perfume."

"I like it!" Corsair grinned. "I don't think the captain and your brother will be as enthused, but we'll get them to come around. What sort of spells were you thinking? The only one of that type Kohar uses is a charm we can put on dangerous animals when we find them, so we can keep tracking them if they get away from us, but it doesn't usually come to that."

"They're all pretty similar, just more elaborate," Taniel replied. "Let me get the right book, and I'll show you."

It was stupid to feel so excited, but he couldn't help it. There was never anybody who wanted to see his work, his ideas. Even Kohar, for all he was genuinely interested, just didn't care about the same esoteric things that Taniel did.

Tracking and finding spells weren't esoteric, but it was still *something*. Better than writing in his own blood in the dead of night while everyone stared on silently horrified, wishing they were anywhere else.

He combed through his books, pulled out the few he wanted, and carried them to the table. Spreading them out, he flipped to the pages he needed in each and then gestured to them all. "These are what I'm going to use. At least four, up to seven depending on time and resources. By the time he finds them all, he'll be certain he's got them and won't look further for anything else."

"So what do you need for all of these?"

"Inks that I thankfully already possess. One I need to make. Items to hold the spells—tokens, coins, even a button will work. The more varied, the better, but it will have to be stuff I wear all the time, so I don't accidentally leave one behind."

"What if he grabs you while you're asleep?"

"Some bits of jewelry will cover that, a bracelet and earring maybe. I'm sure I've got something suitable around here." Taniel walked off again, this time to his wardrobe, where he pulled out the heavy jewelry case he'd inherited when… well, there was no one left but him and Kohar. He'd gotten their father's, and Taniel their mother's.

Carrying it over to the table, he set it between a couple of the books and flipped it open. Over the years, some pieces he'd given away as gifts or sold to help fund his studies, but he'd kept all the important pieces and acquired a few as well.

He rifled delicately through the mess, which had been organized and tidy once but not suffered hard, fast travel well, and he'd yet to feel like sitting down and fixing it. Eventually, he turned up what he was looking for: an old pair of silver hoops, each threaded with a tiny emerald bead, and a leather bracelet woven with beads of bone and metal. It had been left behind by a visitor who'd never returned to reclaim it, so Taniel had taken it after their one-year waiting period.

He'd hate to lose it, but it was perfect for this plan. The earrings were a pair his mother had always hated but had come from a relative, so she hadn't been able to get rid of them either. She'd be pleased they were being put to such a use, even if she'd also beat his ass for all the stupid choices that had led to this moment.

"Everything all right?"

"Huh?" Taniel looked up. "Oh, yes, it's fine.

This box and most of its contents belonged to my mother. Hard not to think about her. I think these will do for two of the spells. Five to go." He went to retrieve his cloak and removed the cloak pin. "Three." He added it to the little pile on the table.

"What about your knife?" Corsair asked, nodding at the knife Taniel always carried for magic and general survival should he get lost out in the woods or some such. "A little obvious, but practical."

"Good idea." Taniel added it to the pile. He sat down to warm a bit by the nearby fire, and his eyes landed on his boots, which had metal buckles to further secure the laces. One of those would work exceedingly well. He removed his boots and added one to the pile, then went to fetch slippers so his toes wouldn't freeze. "Up to five now, just need—" He broke off with a cry as his slipper caught on a rough patch in the floor and sent him stumbling right out of them.

To land awkwardly in Corsair's lap like a wench at a bar. "Oh, good grief! I'm so sorry!" Face burning, he squirmed up and away, then gathered up his backstabbing slippers and went to throw them in the back of the wardrobe where they now belonged. In their place, he pulled out the ugly shoes he'd once worn at the monastery, kept for days when he needed a pair of shoes he didn't care about ruining.

Wishing vainly that he was dead, he dragged himself back over to the table. "Sorry again for being such a clumsy fool."

Corsair laughed and smiled at him. "Clumsy is how often your brother falls down the stairs he uses every single day. That aside, I've never had complaints when pretty men or women fall into my lap."

"I'm fairly certain it was less fall and more crash, but I'm glad you're not traumatized by the event," he replied, not stupid enough to get his hopes up that

Corsair's reply had been intentionally flirty. He was just trying to make Taniel feel better.

Corsair's smile turned mischievous. "Only disappointed it ended too soon."

All right, *that* was definitely flirting. Taniel didn't remotely trust his good luck. "Since when do you flirt with me?"

"Since you accidentally offered to ride me this morning," Corsair replied. "You always seemed hung up on your ex, even if he is a bastard. Also, you're Kohar's brother, which is a death sentence if I screw up."

Taniel deflated. "Yes, always Kohar's brother."

"I didn't mean it like that," Corsair replied, rolling to his feet like a cat and crossing the room to him. He tilted Taniel's chin up with one finger. "I mean that if I hurt you, I also hurt your family. Goes both ways, you know. Think my five siblings and twenty-seven cousins and god knows how many half cousins thrice removed would come for your head if you did something to hurt me?"

"I do know a bit about large families and their vendettas, yes," Taniel drawled. "I'm the poor little orphan boy. What do you think happened when *anybody* picked on me? Allowances were spent on bail, that's what."

Corsair snickered and slowly withdrew his finger. "If you can ever bear to talk more about them, I'd love to hear your stories. They sound like they would have gotten along well with my family. Probably too well." He stepped back slightly, which was disappointing, but probably reasonable, even if Taniel couldn't come up with why.

"Also, given what we're doing, it's not really the right time to be flirting. We've a killer to hunt, and I can't imagine how difficult it is for you, given how much you cared about him."

Taniel laughed bitterly and walked past him to the table to get back to work. "I stopped caring about Vosgi the moment he looked me in the eye and said he'd put what remained of my family down in the ground with the rest of them. He said he loved me, and then he said that." He didn't start crying, but it was a near thing, remembering the hate in Vosgi's face, the venom in his eyes, the ice-cold certainty of his vow. It had been like staring at a stranger, until Taniel realized—admitted—the stranger had been the man pretending to love him. This Vosgi was the real one.

He startled slightly as arms wrapped around him from behind, and the tears did spill then, abruptly and wholly without permission. He'd thought he was handling everything so well, but maybe it was more difficult than he'd been admitting. "Thank you."

Corsair squeezed him even tighter for a moment, then let go and returned to his chair. "I know a bit about feeling all alone in the world, even when people who know me are right there. So what should we use for the last two—"

A pounding at the door drowned out the rest of his words, and Taniel rolled his eyes as Corsair went to answer it.

To no one's surprised, Kohar spilled inside, his long, long hair a tangled, windswept mess around him, snow still covering it and nearly all the rest of him. "You're finally awake."

"Despite my best efforts," Taniel replied. "Why do you look like someone pushed you into the snow."

In the doorway, dismissing a couple of soldiers who'd come with them, Nerek snorted. "He pushed himself, as is his tendency."

"Oh, shut up," Kohar grumbled as he stripped off his sodden outer layers and went to stand by the fire.

"It's not my fault the snow was hiding a giant ass rock."

Nerek chuckled and sat down in the seat nearest Corsair. "So what have you two been up to?"

Taniel laid out the plan they'd come up with, stopping only when a servant arrived with food and drink. Though he'd just eaten not long ago, he was more than happy to eat again as he finished his explanation.

"Should weave a charm into your hair," Kohar said. "At the nape, where it's not easily seen. He'll be really pleased with himself for finding that one, and it's another piece you'll have on you at all times." He didn't wait for Taniel's reply, simply started rifling through the jewelry case himself, muttering and laughing occasionally. "Did you sell those ugly frogs?"

"Of course I did. Those things were terrifying. Let someone else suffer them."

Kohar snickered again, and then finally came up with a small hair charm in the shape of a rose, carved from wood and gleaming in the flickering light. "Perfect." He added it to the pile. "One more. It's a really good plan, Tani, even if I hate the idea of you being bait. Hopefully it won't take us long to get to you."

Taniel's brows rose into his hairline. "I thought you'd yell at me some more."

Kohar's gaze flicked ever so briefly to Nerek, then back to Taniel. "Yelling just seems to go in one ear and out the other with you. There's no denying you know Vosgi best, anyway. Just seriously: don't get dead. I'll never forgive you."

"I know. I'll be careful. I don't want to die, you know. Quite the opposite."

"Then let's find number seven and get to work."

It was Nerek who said, "Your belt buckle."

"Perfect!" Taniel said, and added his belt to the pile. "Now comes the hard part."

Kohar rolled his eyes. "Hard. Please. This is light work for you. Do you need/want help, or shall I leave you to it?"

"Help would be nice," Taniel said with a smile. "I like when we work on magic together."

Kohar smiled back and scooped up the chosen tokens to carry them across the room to Taniel's work station. "All right. Let me go to my room and get what I need, and I'll be back shortly." He departed, Nerek right behind him.

"Shortly my ass," Taniel said. "Only if Nerek gets called away."

Corsair snickered. "I wasn't going to say it, but I was definitely thinking it. So what does putting magic in these items entail?"

"We'll have to write out the spells on special paper, then wrap the objects in them, one piece to each object. After that, we finish the spells and hope it takes. Some items are more resistant than others to being spelled, and one slip in the writing can cause all kinds of disasters."

"Kohar was right though, wasn't he? This is light work for you."

Taniel shrugged. "All magic is hard work, unless you're a cocky asshole bent on murder. But yes, relatively speaking, charming tokens isn't the hardest work I've done."

"You're so cocky at times, and so modest at others," Corsair replied with a laugh. "Why not just admit you're leagues ahead of Kohar? It's not like he'd be angry or deny it. Even before you arrived, he mentioned you were way better than him."

"I don't know." Taniel shrugged. "It's weird when you're the little orphan boy who copies your whole life. Fine. Yes." He lifted his head and jutted his chin out. "I'm leagues better than Kohar. He's a sad, pale imitation of me, so there."

Corsair's sly grin returned. "Not very convincing. I've seen you cockier."

"Maybe I'm not in the mood." Maybe he didn't want to start sounding like Vosgi. What if he hadn't turned them in? Would he have just kept going? Would he have turned into Vosgi at some point? Gone gleefully along with his real plans, whatever they had been? Whatever they might still be? Taniel liked to think no, he'd never do such a thing, but he hadn't thought he'd fall into infatuation with a lying, murderous cretin either.

"I'm cocky enough for six anyway," Corsair replied. He closed the distance between them and chucked Taniel's chin playfully. "I have to get some sleep and see what Nerek needs from me, but if I were to drop by in the dead hours of the morning again…"

"Drop by and find out."

"Looking forward to it." Grinning, Corsair rested a hand ever so briefly against his cheek, letting it fall away slowly, and then headed off, leaving Taniel alone.

Sighing, tired and overexcited all at once, Taniel put his attention and energy to work setting up his stations for the hours of work ahead of him.

Thankfully, he had the vast majority of the inks. There was only one he'd need to make. He'd start with that, because it would need time to set, which he could use to write out the other spells.

Puttering around the work area, he got everything into his little table cauldron and gently simmering. Keeping a careful eye on it, he drew up a stool and set to work thoroughly cleaning each of the talismans.

The door opened as he was finishing the earrings and moving on to the bracelet. "Sooner than I expected. Thought for sure Nerek would take longer."

"Shut up," Kohar said cheerfully. "Don't think I haven't noticed how you've been eying his second-in-command."

"I have no idea what you're talking about," Taniel retorted, the back of his neck burning. "Stop running your mouth and get to work."

Kohar rolled his eyes but did so, setting out his own inks and other supplies on the opposite side of the large table where Taniel did most of his work.

He hadn't expected a position when he'd arrived at Castle Rehm. He'd expected a whole lot of people to rightfully hate and blame him. He'd expected Kohar to be kind, but to eventually send him on his way.

Instead, he got a room of his own, a job he genuinely liked and was good at, and a big, loud, active castle to enjoy. So much like their old life back in the city, but just different enough not to be a constant, painful reminder of everything they'd lost.

As he finished cleaning all the tokens, he set each one on a clean piece of cloth. Rough homespun, but clean and unmarred, so they'd stay that way until the casting. Even just a smidge of dirt could throw everything off, and gods forbid something like blood got in the way.

By the time he was done arranging them, his ink had reached the next stage. He added carefully measured amounts from his bottles of powders and liquids, each one prepared at great effort or acquired at significant cost.

When it had turned a rich, vibrant blue, he fanned the flames to get it hotter, until the mixture was a rolling boil. After that he had to watch it closely, until it just barely started to turn green. Then he promptly removed it from the flames, added a sprig of lavender, and carried it to a window to sit in the freezing cold to set.

"Well done," Kohar said as he returned. "That's not one I have to make often, and I invariably screw up the timing at least once. Mom and Dad would brag about you constantly if they were still around."

For no good reason at all, Taniel suddenly wanted to cry again. He managed to laugh instead, though it came about a bit wobbly. "I think they'd just say it's nice that I've taken after you so well."

Kohar frowned but didn't say anything, though Taniel had a feeling it was only a matter of time. He'd have to make Kohar forget about the stupid comment. What was wrong with him lately? He was usually much better about keeping his stupid thoughts to himself.

Hopefully everything would get better once he finally dealt with Vosgi.

With that in mind, he pulled up his stool again, sat down, and began to write out the first of the spells. Across from him, Kohar did the same, the two of them working together in congenial silence broken only by the wind outside and the crackling of the fire.

Several hours later, they at last finished. "I don't think I've ever done so much work in one session," Taniel said around a yawn, slumping over his worktable and letting his eyes fall closed for just a few minutes. "Let's never do that again."

"Agreed," Kohar said from where he was sprawled on a nearby settee. "Wake me up when it's time to look them over."

Taniel just grunted and forced himself to his feet. Stumbling over to his bed, he discarded his shoes and most of his clothes, then burrowed beneath the blankets and promptly fell asleep.

He woke a few hours later, to judge by the lack of light as he dragged his eyes open, to the smell of roasted meat and spiced wine, the soft rattle and clink of someone arranging the meal. Yawning, he reluctantly shoved back his warm blankets and sat up—and froze in surprise. "What are you doing here?"

Corsair laughed. "You told me to 'find out,' didn't you? What I found was you dead asleep. Figured food wouldn't hurt. Didn't mean to wake you."

"You didn't," Taniel replied. "Thank you for the food."

"How did the spell work go?" Corsair asked, pouring them both wine before taking a seat nearby, leaving the laden table entirely to Taniel. "I saw Kohar briefly on his way to his room, and last I heard he was still dead asleep. I almost didn't think you'd wake until morning."

Taniel shrugged. "I don't usually need as much rest as most seem to, though my comparison was usually a bunch of old, crotchety monks who hated having to do anything that wasn't illuminating or bundling herbs."

"Well, you recover faster than Kohar." Corsair winked. "To judge by how much he sleeps when he's done… working… anyway."

Taniel nearly spat out his wine, then nearly spilled it as he tried to set it down. "I'm going to use that as blackmail later."

Corsair's grin was slow and full of mischief. "That's not nice. What if I paid generously for you not to do that?"

Gods above, Corsair flirting so brazenly was going to destroy what little brain Taniel possessed. "That would depend on how generous."

"Come find out."

Though Taniel had only taken a few bites of his

dinner, all thoughts of food had completely fled his mind. Pushing back his chair, he rose and took the few steps to where Corsair was sitting closer to the fire. Thank goodness he hadn't bothered to put all his discarded clothes back on; all he'd retained was his hose and under robe, which already felt like too much.

Corsair spread his legs and reached out as Taniel stood between them, running his hands along his thighs and around to cup his ass. "Feels as delightful as it's always looked."

"Where did you learn to flirt? A tavern?"

"The army," Corsair replied with a laugh, and tugged gently, urging Taniel to lean down, which he was more than happy to do. He slid his fingers into Corsair's soft, beautiful hair and tilted his head up, so they met halfway, sighing whisper soft as he finally got a taste of that mouth he'd been spinning fantasies about for so long.

Corsair kissed playfully at first, flirting touches and flicks of his tongue, the barest tease of teeth, before he finally kissed in earnest, tongue pushing into Taniel's mouth to explore and conquer, sharing the flavor of mulled wine and the thrill of a new lover.

Tearing away, licking his lips, Taniel said, "Maybe we should try this in a more comfortable arrangement."

Eyes shining, Corsair nudged him back enough to stand, then ushered Taniel over to the bed. Taniel hit the edge of it and sat, and this time it was his turn to have Corsair between his thighs. He liked that lots and lots. "You're wearing entirely too many clothes."

"Then get them off," Corsair replied, and started the process by removing his belt and stripping off his outer tunic. After that went his under tunic, followed by him sitting down next to Taniel to remove his boots and hose.

Discarding his own minimal clothes, Taniel climbed further into the bed and sprawled out. As Corsair turned, Taniel reached out and dragged him close, not quite moaning as he finally got Corsair right where he'd always wanted him. "You're beautiful." He smoothed his hands along Corsair's shoulders, down his chest to playfully grip at the trim hips. "I didn't think you even noticed me."

"A dead man would notice you, Taniel," Corsair replied, and pushed him down into the bedding before pressing all that lovely weight against him and kissing him breathless, cock rubbing against his skin, leaving damp trails and hinting at all the delights still to come. "I really hope you meant it about riding me, because I haven't been able to get the image out of my head."

"Oh, I meant it."

Corsair whimpered then and kissed him wet and messy before tearing away and setting to work mapping Taniel's body with mouth and hands. Taniel tried to get in some touching of his own, but mostly he was reduced to digging his nails into Corsair's skin, enjoying the softness of it, the ripple of muscles, as Corsair took him apart one incendiary touch at a time.

"Please, damn it," he finally howled. "If you want me to ride you, let me do it."

Chuckling in a way that did nothing whatsoever to calm Taniel down, Corsair grabbed hold and reversed their positions. Taniel groaned and moved away long enough to get the lubricant he needed, then returned and set to work prepping himself, enjoying the groans and curses that got him. Using what remained on his slick hands, he stroked Corsair's cock thoroughly before rising up and lining everything up. The hands on his hips were almost painfully tight, but the look in Corsair's eyes as he watched was vastly more captivating.

Taniel moaned as he finally sank down. "You feel even better than I imagined."

"Was going to say the same thing," Corsair said with a strained laugh. "Let's go, mage. Show me what you can do."

Grinning, Taniel did as told, rising up and shoving back down, taking Corsair as deep as he possibly could. The hands on his hips were tighter than ever, and sweat dripped down his face, stinging his eyes, as he worked Corsair's cock in earnest, moving up and down, hips rolling, panting breaths filling the air. Firelight glowed on Corsair's skin and flickered in his hungry eyes as he urged Taniel on, keeping pace with his movements.

As Corsair finally got a hand around his cock and stroked it firm and quick, Taniel came apart with a cry. Corsair gripped his hips again, rolled them over, and fucked him with a last few, hard thrusts before spilling inside him, moans muffled in the hollow of Taniel's throat.

Panting heavily, Corsair rolled off him and moved to sprawl on the bed, head on a borrowed pillow. Taniel stretched out next to him, savoring the burn of well-used muscles and the stickiness between his thighs that proved how much Corsair had enjoyed the ride.

"Am I free of the blackmail, then?" Corsair asked.

Taniel laughed into his pillow and turned his head to say, "I'm pretty sure blackmail is all about seeing how much I can get out of you for as long as possible."

"Oh, I see how it is." He laughed. "Brat. Go finish your meal, and afterward I'll provide the next payment."

"See? The blackmail is working splendidly for me already."

Corsair grinned evilly and didn't otherwise reply.

Skin prickling with anticipation, Taniel dug a robe out of his wardrobe and went to finish his food, which thankfully was still delicious cold.

He'd nearly finished when a loud, terrifying clanging sound filled the air. Before he could ask what in the name of the gods the racket was about, Corsair had thrown himself out of bed and was gathering up his clothes. "That's the fire alarm for the village! I've got to go; I'll see you there." He yanked his boots on, grabbed his belt, and bolted from the room.

Taniel stood so quickly his chair fell over and bolted for his wardrobe. Yanking on clothes, pulling on his boots and lacing them as quickly as possible, he then fetched all his equipment, buckling and strapping everything into place as he headed out.

In the courtyard, a horse waited for him, along with a trio of guards. All around him, people were working frantically, gearing up and heading out in waves. Off in the distance, an eerie orange light bled across the night sky.

He had a sinking feeling he knew who was responsible for a massive fire in the dead of winter. Thankfully, he'd grabbed his newly-spelled items, along with everything else. Buckling the last of his equipment into place and securing the charm that went in his hair, right at the nape of his neck as Kohar had suggested, Taniel left his room and headed through the castle

Out in the yard, he mounted his horse and turned it to the gate. "Where's Kohar?"

"Already headed out with the captain," one of the guards said. "Captain said we're to stay with you, keep you safe, as he suspects the worst about the fire."

Taniel didn't bother to reply, just gave his horse the signal and rode off into the night, bound for the village as quickly as he dared in the ice and snow.

They arrived to a nightmare: flames, smoke, screaming and wailing. The smell was horrendous, and the heat unbearable. Taniel set to work anyway, pulling out potions and charms, incantations that only needed the last couple of words before they flared to life.

He swore at one point he could hear Kohar's voice, and he caught the barest glimpse of Corsair before everything was lost once again to a haze of casting spells and helping people. Somewhere in the mess, he lost his bodyguards, though that wasn't their fault. He hoped Nerek didn't blame them later.

People walked in a shambling line toward the castle, guided by Bedros, Warren, and most of the staff of the castle. Everyone else was fighting the fire; thankfully, they seemed to be turning the tide.

Taniel braced himself against the wall of a stone shed that was far enough from the conflagration to escape destruction, and fumbled out a few more slips of unfinished spells, rubbing at his eyes as they blurred. Shoving his spectacles back into place, he wrote out the missing bits of spell, then balled the bits of paper up, activated, and threw.

More fires went out, or at least dampened, allowing others to move in and put them out for good.

Taniel moved on to the next. And the next. Until his eyes wouldn't cooperate, and he couldn't seem to find more flames anyway.

Someone called his name, and Taniel turned, trying to find the source of the voice—and slipped on a patch of ice that somehow had survived all the fire around them, going down hard, landing in the cold and wet. He tried to stand up, especially when the voice came more frantically, but suddenly it was all just too much effort.

He really needed to not make a habit of collapsing dramatically in the snow, but it was so cold, and he was so hot…

Taniel woke with a start and groaned as a stabbing pain in his head immediately made itself known. Everything smelled of smoke, which wasn't helping. Swearing, he fumbled away the blankets covering him, sitting up and forcing his eyes open all at once.

Not the castle. A house that was singed but not too severely damaged. So still in the village. That was good. It meant the village was still somewhat standing and that Vosgi hadn't taken him yet… Which seemed strange, because the fire must have been set to get him out in the open where Vosgi could snatch him.

Well, he wouldn't get answers to his questions by sitting around. His whole body ached, especially his stupid head, but he'd rest later. Heaving to his feet, stomach roiling in time with his throbbing head, Taniel set off.

Outside, the village was bursting with activity. Cleaning, tending wounded, cooking… right in the middle of the fray, keeping everything running smoothly, was Bedros, with Warren nearby.

Taniel fought tears as he looked over the ruin. His fault. This was all his fault. If Vosgi wasn't mad at him, he'd never have come here to hurt and kill people. Destroy their homes. Leave them living in fear of what would happen next.

He never should have come. It was long past time for him to go. The minute Vosgi was dead, that was exactly what he was going to do.

That still left the question of why Vosgi hadn't grabbed him while he'd had the chance. Maybe the fire had worked too well, and Vosgi hadn't been able to find him in the mayhem. Which meant he may be skulking about right now.

Well, nothing he could do except be on guard. He was so wrung out from helping with the fire, he wouldn't be able to put up much of a fight. At least their plan was in place.

He looked around again, this time for a familiar face he could interrupt without causing problems. As he stepped further into the street, however, and people noticed him, everyone seemed to falter, some even stop, and a murmur swept through the crowd that Taniel didn't like remotely. The tone was angry, scared.

"I'm sorry," he said to no one in particular. He needed to find his brother or Nerek.

He went right, which seemed as good a direction as any, but hadn't gotten more than perhaps ten steps when someone shouted, "You!"

Taniel turned, and before he could get a word out, a large, burly man who looked a lot like Corsair punched him, then grabbed him and slammed him into the wall of the nearest house, sending ashes and lingering smoke up in a cloud around them. Taniel coughed and wheezed, choking out, "What?

"You! Nothing but trouble, and now Cori's gone because of you!"

"Cori? Corsair? Let me—" Taniel cried out in pain as the man slammed him into the wall again, and threw up as he was dropped to the ground like a sack of flour. "I don't understand— Stop!" He shouted as someone else, maybe two someones, kicked and hit him. "Stop! Please! I don't know what's going on. Explain the problem to me before you beat me to death." He scrabbled at the wall, managed to heave himself to his feet, but only because a handful of people had come up and dragged the bigger man back. The two who'd joined in to help him withdrew as well, but clearly they were ready for any excuse whatsoever to resume the beating. "What's going on?" Gods he really needed his head to stop hurting.

A tall, handsome woman with gray hair and Corsair's eyes joined the group, and Taniel had the miserable, sinking feeling he knew what was going on. Before he could ask, the woman said, "He took Corsair. That stupid, evil bastard *you* brought here took my son! He was supposed to take you!"

Taniel flinched. "I'm sorry, I don't know—it *was* supposed to be me, I don't know why Vosgi would take Corsair instead. I'll find him and bring him back, I promise."

The woman scoffed. "You've been vowing to stop that bastard for months now, and look where that's got us. I can tell you this: if my son dies, you'll die worse. Let's go, we've got work to do."

Slowly, the men who'd assaulted him followed the woman—mother and brothers? Cousins? Mix of both?—down the street and out of sight, and the rest of the crowd trickled back to their own various tasks.

Taniel swallowed, scrubbed at his eyes, and resumed his attempts to find Kohar. If he hadn't been certain leaving was the right thing before, he knew it was now.

Thankfully, he heard Kohar after a bit and followed his familiar shouting to the south edge of the village, where he was ranting at length about… something… Taniel didn't have the energy to sort out the particulars. "Kohar! Enough! Your yelling isn't helping anybody. Do you even know what you're yelling about anymore? Knock it off."

Kohar whipped around, and his sooty, scratched, and bloody face filled with relief. "Taniel! You're awake!" He rushed over and hugged him tightly. "How are you feeling?"

"Been better, been worse. What's this about Vosgi taking Corsair?"

"I see you've already heard," Kohar said, mouth flattening. "He found you lying on the ground, out cold. Brought you to safety and went to get help and… that's it. He never reached anyone to ask for help, never went back to you. No one has seen him, and there's no hint anywhere of where he could be. So we've assumed the worst."

Taniel's eyes stung and blurred. "He was supposed to take *me*."

"We don't know that's what happened, though on that note, be careful, because his family is understandably upset and liable to lash out at the first person they can find to blame."

Sniffling, Taniel wiped his eyes and said, "Yeah, they already introduced me to a wall and issued a death threat. It's fine," he added when Kohar bristled like a cat. "You'd do the same thing in their position, don't try to say otherwise. I'm going to go look for clues, because if Vosgi did take him, he'll have left something behind that only I would understand or be able to see."

Kohar looked desperately like he wanted to argue, from the many expressions that flickered across his face as he struggled to come up with a sound argument, but at last sighed, shoulders slumping. "Fine. The minute you figure something out though, come back here so we can form a plan, all right?"

"Fine," Taniel echoed.

Giving him a look their mother would have been proud of, Kohar said, "Promise."

"I promise."

"Get to work, then."

Taniel nodded, hugged him briefly one last time, and then headed back to the cabin where he'd been recovering to get his things. Thankfully, they were in fact there, since it hadn't occurred to him until the last moment that they could have been put somewhere else. He slung the satchel across his chest and headed for the door—and then stopped.

One by one he removed all the charms he and Kohar had worked so hard on. Nobody else was going to be put at risk. Not anymore. They'd suffered enough. They should never have suffered at all.

Dumping them on the bed, he restored his outer wear and satchel and finally headed out. His headache had lessened slightly, but his stomach growled, reminding him how long it had been since he'd last eaten and all the energy he'd expended with his magic.

Food and a strong cup of tea would do him a world of good. Looking around, though, all he saw was a sea of suspicious and hostile glares. He didn't dare ask where he could get something to eat. Even if they were willing to help him, did he really deserve it?

The rations he always kept in his bag would have to suffice, though it was just jerky and water, which didn't amount to much. Better than nothing.

Shoulders hunched, he slid his spectacles into place and set to searching carefully through the ruined village.

Thankfully, it didn't take long to find what he was looking for. On the back of a shed that had just barely escaped the inferno, painted in a combination of blood and spell ink to make it invisible to the naked eye, was a crude map. Northwest, further into the mountains, to what looked like a small valley, or maybe a gulch, hard to say. Drawing out paper and pencil, he copied the map down as quickly as he could without sacrificing accuracy. This would be a lot easier if he could ask a local for help, but he didn't feel like getting his nose broken.

He also didn't want to risk anyone insisting on coming with him or ratting him out to Kohar.

This was *his* fault, and *he* would fix it. Stowing everything but the map, bundling his cloak tightly around him, Taniel headed off into the woods, the sounds of the village rapidly fading. Soon, his only company was the howling wind and the biting snow it kicked up in his face. Thankfully, that same wind was making quick work of erasing his tracks, so even when Kohar realized Taniel was a promise-breaking liar, he wouldn't be able to follow.

Morning turned to afternoon as he pressed on, stopping only when he needed rest or his head simply hurt too much to keep going. He really wished he'd been able to get some food; the small bundle of emergency jerky he kept in his bag just wasn't sufficient.

Stupid Vosgi. All the trouble they'd gone to, and he'd thwarted them by simply kidnapping a completely different person.

He sat down on a large boulder to catch his breath and go over the map. Dead ahead was the large tree noted on the map as a landmark. He was nearly there. A couple more hours of hiking through this stupid snow and he'd be there.

If only he had any idea about what he'd be facing, other than Vosgi at his nastiest and meanest. What if he'd already hurt Corsair? Or already…

Taniel couldn't even bear to think it.

Ugh, his head. He was not in fighting shape. Maybe he should have risked the broken nose after all. Or just had Kohar get the food for him, that would have been smart. Oh, well. Too late now. He wolfed down more jerky, tucked the remainder away, and heaved to his feet.

Snow was falling gently now, the wind having quieted some for the moment. This far up, they weren't likely to stumble across his tracks, so he was well and truly alone. He was so tired of being alone. For all he sometimes felt overlooked, he'd still never doubted his family loved him, had never considered him anything but a real member of the family. Ever since they'd died…

Vosgi really had seen a weakness and preyed upon it ruthlessly. Taniel had been a gullible fool desperate for any scraps of love and affection, that sense of belonging the plague had taken from him. Now, because of his own weakness and stupidity, he was going to be alone again.

Assuming, of course, he survived.

Would it be better for everyone if he didn't? No, Kohar would be distraught, even if no one else would miss him. Corsair? Maybe a little bit, before he'd been kidnapped because of Taniel. How did Vosgi even know about him and Corsair? They hadn't done anything where Vosgi would see—they'd barely done anything at all. He didn't even think he could say Corsair was his lover. Certainly not *now.*

Not that it mattered, since the moment Corsair was safely back with his family, Taniel was leaving.

The next landmark was a cluster of boulders that narrowed the path so he'd be walking right along the cliffside. Was Vosgi's plan for him to either exhaust himself to death or fall to his demise? No, neither of those was mean enough to satisfy Vosgi.

For that matter, how had Vosgi gotten up here hauling someone who was either unconscious or hostile? Didn't matter. All that mattered was finding them, killing Vosgi, and getting Corsair home safe.

His stomach growled, and Taniel sighed.

The boulders came into sight, jutting into the path he was walking exactly as the map had indicated, leaving him creeping slowly and carefully, snow crunching, tumbling over the edge in threat and promise of what a single wrong move would cost him.

By the time he cleared the boulders and stumbled onto a safer, wider, well away from the edge path, Taniel was ready to throw up. He'd spent his fair share of time in the mountains, but the monks weren't stupid enough to trek across such dangerous pathways. If it couldn't be done safely, it couldn't be done. If only he'd had more respect for that rule from the start.

Nearly there. The boulder was the final landmark before the destination, which was almost a straight shot from here, just on the other side of the scraggly little stretch of trees and down into the valley or gulch or whatever it was.

When he drew close to the copse, he stopped to sit and rest one more time, tucking down amongst the trees to avoid the worst of the frigid wind that had returned with a vengeance. Pulling out his jerky, he wolfed down the last of it, chasing it with the remaining water in his skin. A last search through his satchel also turned up a small tin of sweets he'd forgotten about, peppermint drops he often sucked on when working. He ate all those too, even if it was still woefully inadequate for whatever he was about to face.

He slid his spectacles back into place, affixing the band that would keep them firmly in place on his head no matter what happened. Though he kept careful watch, looking, looking again, looking thrice, he spied no magical markers, no hints of traps or other nasty surprises.

Odd, to say the least. Also ominous. It meant

Vosgi was saving all his nastiness for one big, ugly blow. No help for it. Taniel pushed on through the scraggly copse of trees, keeping alert all the while, increasingly anxious as all he found was nothing.

Shoving through a particularly nasty tangle of young trees and thorny shrubs, he stumbled into the clearing—and stopped as he saw the figure waiting for him just a few paces away. Taniel licked his lips, dry and chapped from the cold. "Vosgi."

"Taniel."

The stupid bastard was still so heartbreakingly beautiful, like a statue of one of the various demigods had been brought to life, all flawless dark brown skin and long, heavy, dark auburn hair, and those eyes as green as grass and sharp as glass. It had been so pathetically easy to believe this man loved him. The shame of it would haunt Taniel the rest of his life.

"Did you finally grow bored of tormenting and killing all these innocent people?"

Vosgi just chuckled, low and mean. "Is that all you have to ask me?"

"What do you want me to ask? Why are you doing this? Because you're an egotistical bastard who can't handle he was told 'no' for once in his life, and instead of moving on with your life you decided the appropriate reaction is to torture and murder people who never did a single fucking thing wrong to you. What are you really up to? You wouldn't tell me, but it probably involves increasing your power and knowledge and doing something that will get still more people killed. Why did you kidnap Corsair when you could have just kidnapped me and saved all of us a great deal of time and trouble?'"

The mean chuckle turned into an outright laugh, as cutting as stepping on shards of glass with bare feet. "I actually meant to just pick one of the children.

They're always running amuck, and no one pays nearly as much attention to them as they should, even in the midst of their homes burning down. Then they have the nerve to get upset when one goes missing." He laughed again. "Then I saw your lovely little collapse, Taniel, and the way that soldier shouted your name, carried you so gently, like he doesn't know your pretty face hides a craven backstabber."

"Your spell was going to get people killed!" Taniel snarled. "I couldn't do that. Everything else, fine. You know I loved the magic, but I wasn't okay with killing people. I'm sorry that offends you, except I'm not really. So where is Corsair and what do you want? Are those the questions you wanted me to ask?"

Vosgi just laughed again. Taniel *hated* that laugh, as much as he'd once thought it wild and free and delightful. He'd been a fucking fool. "I don't have your stupid soldier. Is his name really Corsair? How embarrassing for him. Anyway, all I did was put him to sleep, dump him in a barn, and cover him with hay. He'll wake up sometime tomorrow, stumble into what's left of that sad little village, and be perfectly fine. No, I just wanted you to *think* I had him, so you'd save me the trouble of having to drag you all the way up here. As usual, Taniel my darling, you're easy to anticipate."

Easy to manipulate, but Vosgi didn't need to say that: it was pathetically obvious. Taniel wanted to cry. Such a stupid, obvious trick, and he'd fallen for it without hesitation. Damn it, he'd even wondered how Vosgi had managed to get Corsair up here and never followed the thought to its logical conclusion. Gods above, how could he be so stupid? He knew Vosgi better than anyone, but that didn't really seem to matter when Vosgi knew him far better.

Sighing, Taniel finally replied, "Fine, then, let's focus on the only question that really matters: what do you want?"

Vosgi smiled in that slow, incendiary way of his that had first been Taniel's undoing. The only thing he'd liked more than Vosgi's burning ember smiles were his scorching kisses. Thinking about them now just made him nauseous. "The same thing I've always wanted, Taniel darling: You. Just you."

"What in the world is that supposed to mean?" Taniel asked. Never mind it was a fucking lie. He'd been here all along, he'd been back at the fucking monastery, even easier for the taking than he was here. Vosgi had never wanted him. "I'm not special. I was just a good assistant."

"Now, now, you were also a good fuck. I'm sure your little pirate-soldier would agree. Throw me your satchel."

Taniel did so, but only because there was nothing in there that would help him, not that he could get to and use fast enough, anyway. "Stop being tiresome and evasive. It's not like you. What suddenly makes me so special?"

"Come find out," Vosgi said with a purr before he stooped, grabbed the satchel, and threw it back toward the cave several paces behind him.

Taniel rolled his eyes. "Yes, because that doesn't scream 'trap.' Come off it, Vosgi."

Vosgi laughed—and laughed and laughed.

Horrified realization struck Taniel then, but as always, he was just a step behind Vosgi. Those deceptively beautiful eyes flashed just as Taniel took a step backward—too late, too late, he was always too fucking late.

The trap activated, confining him to a circle of earth just clear of the tree line. Taniel screamed, pain like knives shooting through him, because his poor body hadn't endured enough already. He dropped to his knees, focusing on his breathing. "What is the *point* of this? If you want to break my stupid seals to free your damned demon, this is the worst possible way to go about it."

That smug laugh washed over him as Vosgi crouched in front of him, close but well clear of the circle—not that Taniel could have reached beyond it to punch him in his stupid face anyway. "The demon is just something to pass the time. It'll keep. Do you really think your silly little seals would stop me for long if I wanted them gone? Please. I've still got one or two vials of your blood left."

"One or two…" Suddenly all the nights he got extremely tired after working or rolling in the sheets made a lot more sense. He'd just chalked it up to hard work and hard play, but clearly he would never truly appreciate the depths of his own gullibility. "You stole my blood? To what purpose? You hardly need my…"

Anger flashed in Vosgi's eyes.

"Oh, my gods, you do," Taniel said, bottom dropping out of his stomach. "You're not more powerful than me. You've been *stealing* from me, and that's why you want me ba…"

One after another, the realizations kept coming.

The spell that had torn them apart, the one that had been the final straw for Taniel, had been a power draw. Vosgi had never said who he was going to steal power from, and Taniel had never asked because he'd just assumed it would be one of the Brothers that Vosgi really hated, or someone from the village where they did most of their trading. He'd been more afraid that if it worked, Vosgi would never stop.

Vosgi had been after him all along, right from the start. "I really never meant anything to you at all, did I? You were going to kill me from day one."

"You've always been precious to me, Taniel

darling. Like the prize cow at the county fair. Unlike the cows all these farmers molest, though, you were also a good lay. We had fun, until you betrayed me. I would have made it painless for you, but I'm afraid that's not an option anymore. Like always, you brought this on yourself."

"Whatever," Taniel replied. "Can we just get it over with, or am I going to have to listen to you yammer for another hour?"

Vosgi laughed as he rose. "Your mouth, Taniel. It's your best and worst quality. If you kept it shut more often, somebody would find you perfect."

Nobody would ever find him perfect. Near as he could tell, nobody even found him tolerable, except the sibling who'd known him all Taniel's life, and even Kohar would probably be better off with Taniel gone again.

Damn it, he wasn't going to cry.

Thankfully, Vosgi had vanished into the cave across the small field. Taniel bowed his head, tears dripping into the snow. Maybe this was what he deserved for once helping Vosgi. For making so many stupid mistakes. Clearly his birth parents had known he wasn't going to be worth the trouble. Too bad for everyone else they hadn't figured out the same thing.

*Everyone else...*

Sniffling, wiping his face, Taniel studied the circle he was strapped in. However worthless he might be, he had power enough that Vosgi wanted to steal it—and Vosgi with a permanent increase in power, instead of just using Taniel's blood for temporary bursts, would be a living nightmare.

He'd have to feel sorry for himself later, because if he just rolled over and gave up now, even more people were going to die. No more innocents were going to die because he was weak and stupid and pathetic.

Think. He had to think. He was trapped in a circle. He couldn't break out of it. He couldn't alter it.

He could make his own, though. Taniel glanced toward the cave entrance, but all was still. Vosgi must be preparing the final components. That didn't give him much time, especially since he'd wasted some of it whining, but he still had *some*.

No satchel, though, which meant none of his spell inks. Blood had always worked fine in a pinch, though. Hopefully he hadn't lost too much dealing with the fire in the village. At least he'd eaten all that jerky and candy, though the combination of dried, salty meat and sweet peppermint wasn't leaving his stomach very happy.

All right. So what could he do? Something small, that Vosgi wouldn't notice beneath all his own work, but it had to be effective. It had to have *punch*.

It had to work, even if it took Taniel too.

Which really made the solution pretty obvious.

Moving to the edge of the circle, as close as he could possibly get, Taniel cleared away the snow until he had smooth, hard ground to work with. Next, he bit down hard on his left hand, until tears streamed down his face and blood pooled in his palm and dripped down the side. Using the middle finger of his right hand, he started by drawing a circle to contain his own spell. The circle he was trapped in shivered, stung, but Vosgi had only spelled it to prevent tampering. There was nothing the spell could do about the ring of enclosure he'd cast on this side of it.

Vosgi had made a mistake, and Taniel was going to make him regret it.

When the casting circle was set, he reopened the wound on his hand and set to work on the spell itself, casting his eyes frequently to the cave.

Thankfully, he finished it without incident before the frozen ground absorbed his blood. All that remained was the very last little piece to bring it to life.

Hopefully this stupid little trick would work. Taniel shoved all the snow back into place, roaming the circle he was trapped in to muss everything up, like he'd been looking for weaknesses, a way out, so Vosgi would miss the only thing that mattered.

He'd just sat down again, knees pulled to his chest in the sulkiest pose he could think of, when Vosgi finally returned, the wind sending his beautiful hair flying up around him, a slash of dark against the snow.

"Thank you for waiting," Vosgi said as he reached the edge of the circle and set down the crude wooden tray he carried, arrayed with an assortment of bottles, bowls, and other tools. Back in the monastery, those tools had been glass and crystal and delicate porcelain. They'd made the inks together, mixed in with all their other projects, easily missed by the rest of the Brothers. It had been so much stupid fun, having their secrets right beneath everyone's nose. Sneaking off to enjoy forbidden kisses and forbidden magic.

Gods he was stupid.

Everything on the tray was ominously familiar for another reason: these were all the components of the spell that Vosgi had been so desperately eager to try. The one that had been a step too far for Taniel. He'd just never realized, fool that he was, that he was the intended victim.

Well, the first victim, which was what had really driven home that he needed to turn them in. Vosgi was never going to be happy killing one person to gain more power. There would always be a reason, an excuse, to go after another. And another.

"Shall we get started?" Vosgi asked, and from the assortment of items lifted, a single small, glass vial, the kind they'd used to transport medicine to surrounding villages, where they could easily pass it out by doses, instead of forcing everyone to come up one by one to receive it from a larger batch.

Instead of a healing tincture, however, this one contained blood. It was slightly discolored from the spell and herbs that kept it fresh, but clearly blood. Taniel wanted to throw up—and very nearly did when Vosgi unstoppered the vial and threw the contents back like a shot of farmer's homebrew.

His blood. Every time they'd been together had just been another chance to leech away his blood.

Tossing the empty vile aside, lips still red, Vosgi smiled coldly. "Brace yourself, darling, because this next bit is going to hurt." He used a knife to draw quickly and neatly in the hard earth, then tipped ink into the hollowed out letters.

Light flared as the first of Vosgi's spells came to life, and though he'd tried to brace himself for it, Taniel still screamed in agony as the pain overtook him. Because that was all the spell was: pain. Not the paralysis spell he would have expected, frequently used by healers when a patient wouldn't or couldn't hold still.

Just pain. Which meant Vosgi needed his body limber, but also needed him unable to move. Taniel had been depending on that, but it didn't make the pain more bearable. He'd held on to the feeble hope that Vosgi would just render him extremely sleepy but hadn't really believed it.

By the time it came to an end, he was sobbing from the agony. His body felt like he'd been thrown down a mountain and then pounded with additional rocks once he'd reached the bottom. Every time he moved, even just *breathed*, the pain increased, sharp and sudden, leaving him struggling to breath for a moment.

"Step one complete," Vosgi said.

"Fuck you," Taniel gasped out, and with every last scrap of strength remaining in his body, turned onto his side in a way he'd be able to access the very last part of his spell, where he just needed to add one last stroke.

Another small bonus was that in his agonized writhing, he'd torn open the hand he'd bitten into again, probably on a rock or something, which spared him having to figure out how to do that.

He stared up through blurry eyes as Vosgi loomed over him, grabbed his right arm, clearly to spread him out. Now or never.

Fighting back the bile burning in his throat, Taniel heaved up, drew the last curving slash of his spell with the blood dripping down one finger, and cast it.

Flames erupted all around them, scorching hot, adding still more pain to that already induced by Vosgi. Taniel grabbed at Vosgi's robes, his grip feeble, but enough combined with heat and panic to send Vosgi toppling. Taniel dragged himself up, over, pinning Vosgi down with his sheer weight as the flames took them both.

He hoped Kohar would forgive him someday. Corsair and his family. He'd never wanted anyone else to suffer for his mistakes.

Taniel passed out.

*~*~*

He jerked awake sobbing, screaming. Pain, there was so much fucking pain. Everything hurt. Burned. Why was he so hot?

Something was wrong. What?

Vosgi. Where was Vosgi?

Movement caught the corner of his eye, but he

couldn't move, only wait as the movement came close enough to make out. Kohar. He looked tired. Bruised. His mouth was pulled into an angry scowl that was Kohar's way of showing he was worried.

"Go back to sleep, you gigantic pain in my ass," Kohar said, even as he gently placed a hand, soft and cool, on Taniel's scorching forehead.

Taniel tried to reply, but as abruptly as he'd woken, sleep took him again, taking all the lingering pain and misery with it.

He woke less jarringly the second time. Third? Who knew.

Still in pain, but it was far less severe. His body felt weird. Stretched too tight, sore at edges where edges shouldn't be.

He still couldn't move much, but he wasn't sure he'd have the strength to anyway. Taniel settled for looking around. The room was dark, but it was definitely *his* room. In Castle Rehm. He'd been on top of the mountain. How the hells had they found him, let alone gotten him back home?

For that matter, how was he even alive?

The sound of movement caught his attention, and he flicked his eyes toward it, chest giving a painful, twisting lurch as Corsair came into view. He looked well, if tired, and some of the tension and misery bled out of Taniel. That was one thing that had gone right. Hadn't he seen Kohar earlier too? Or had that been a dream?

"You're awake," Corsair said, sitting on the edge of the bed so he faced Taniel. "Kohar said it was the magic and medicines keeping you asleep and you were fine, that you'd woken a couple of times already, but still… I'm glad you're healing up. When we found you…" He shook his head. "Sorry, I shouldn't be dumping all that on you right now."

He reached out and lightly touched Taniel's hand, which felt bandaged. Made sense. He should be little more than ash and charcoal right now. How in the world had he survived? It took a ridiculous amount of effort to lick his dry lips and ask, "How?"

"Worry about that later, you stubborn brat. Right now, focus on healing. Everyone has been worried sick about you. They'll be thrilled to hear you not just woke up, but said a few words. That's great progress."

Taniel was fairly certain one barely coughed out 'how' wasn't the same as 'a few words,' but he wasn't exactly fit to argue. "Water?" he rasped out.

"Of course, and I'll get your latest dose of tonic too." He vanished from view, but returned after only seconds, carrying a cup and a bottle of dark blue glass.

Setting them aside out of view, Corsair then went to the opposite side of the bed and climbed in. Taniel's eyes teared, with pain and relief and a fragile happiness, when Corsair gently lifted his head up to prop it on Corsair's thigh. "Here, tonic first." He tipped the bottle slightly, just enough for a measure of the contents to trickle into Taniel's mouth. It was bitter and salty, but he'd had this tonic, or one very like it, before. If not for it, he'd be in a great deal more pain.

Corsair took the bottle away and replaced it with the cup, giving Taniel tiny sips between generous pauses. He clearly had experience at helping invalids. His thigh was firm and warm beneath Taniel's head, infinitely better than the pillow.

He tried to talk some more, but exhaustion and the pain-dulling tonic were getting the better of him, and he only managed a softly sighed, "Sta…" before he was out again.

*~*~*

The next time he woke, at least the next time he woke long enough to remember it, Taniel almost felt human again. Sore, achy, and full on pain if he moved too quickly, but definitely better.

His room was empty, but judging by the still-steaming food on the table by the fire, the open book by it, someone had only recently been called away. Further good sign that he was on the mend.

With all sorts of questions spinning through his mind. Mostly, how in the world had he managed to live? That fire should have killed him and Vosgi. Hopefully it had half succeeded.

He wouldn't know until he found someone to ask, though. There was sunshine coming in through the cracks between tapestry and window, so it shouldn't be hard to find people. Assuming whoever was watching him didn't return soon.

Moving slowly, wincing at the way every moment pulled at his skin, which felt tight and raw, Taniel eventually made it out of bed. He walked stiffly over to the window and pulled back the tapestry covering it to look outside. The inner yard below was bustling with its usual activity, and he could see smoking chimneys and movement in the village in the distance. Good signs. Hopefully arranging shelter for all the people who'd lost their homes was going well, and they'd be comfortable until spring came and the rebuilding could begin.

Spells for protection whirled through his mind, but Taniel tamped them down. Nobody wanted his help—nobody wanted him, period. Corsair's relatives had made that *very* clear. Once he was really and truly healed up, they'd probably help him pack.

Letting the tapestry fall back into place, he headed across the room to the table, wholly intent on stealing the abandoned meal.

He'd just sat down and pulled the food close when the door creaked open. Taniel jerked around and stared as Corsair stepped into the room. His eyes widened when he realized the bed was empty. "What—" He turned, and the tension bled from his shoulders as he took in Taniel by the fire. "You shouldn't be up!"

"I'm fine." Taniel held up a hand when Corsair started to argue. "Fine enough. I promise."

Corsair crossed the room and swept him up into a hug that made everything hurt, but also made everything better. "You stubborn ass, we all thought you were dead. We didn't know if you'd make it for days, and even then, we weren't sure how you'd be when you woke up." He drew back, let Taniel go, and cupped his face. "Your promises aren't worth shit."

Taniel laughed-cried. "I know. I'm sorry. I just didn't want anyone else getting hurt because of me. Please tell me Vosgi is dead at least."

"There's nothing left of him except some ashes and bits of bone that didn't burn." Corsair slowly withdrew his hands but took hold of one of Taniel's. "You shouldn't have gone up there alone. We nearly didn't get to you in time. If not for—" He broke off and hugged Taniel again. "I'm going to kill you myself. There was so much blood, and you were burned everywhere."

Though he really wanted to stay right where he was, Taniel drew back enough to say, "Tell me what happened. After I… well, after I took care of Vosgi, I remember nothing."

"Sit and eat," Corsair replied, practically shoving Taniel into his vacated seat. He took the opposite seat and sipped at the cup of ale set with the meal. "I woke up in the Macram's barn covered in hay and stumbled my way back to town. Everyone freaked out." His face turned into a thundercloud. "That's when I found out how my family had treated you when they thought you were to 'blame' for my being taken."

Taniel flinched and looked down at the food, stomach queasy now. "They had every right—"

"They had no right!" Corsair said, slamming a fist on the table. "They're better than that, or should be! They certainly raised me to be better than that. Nobody is to blame for any of this except that piece of shit monk. The one you fought, that you faced alone, that you nearly died killing! If they want to act like cretins, then that's how they'll be treated."

Taniel wanted to cry. "Corsair, you and your family are so close. I never meant to cause a rift. They were understandably scared and angry."

"You were hurt, and exhausted from fighting the fire, and just as scared and worried as them, but I didn't see you going around hitting people on the barest excuse. If my family really cares, they'll learn their damn lesson and come apologize. They know how I feel and that I want there to be something between us. So fuck them."

"I want there to be something too," Taniel said, tears finally breaking free. "It feels like I've been nothing but a burden since I arrived. Whatever you and Kohar say, it *is* my fault Vosgi came here and murdered so many people."

Corsair stood, stepped around the table, and pulled Taniel back into his arms. "It's not your fault, Taniel. He would have simply gone to a different village, killed different—"

"No! You don't understand! It was me he wanted the whole time!"

"Kohar figured as much, judging by what was left of the spell he had you trapped in, the implements that were laid out. That still doesn't make it your fault. You're as much a victim as anyone—moreso, in some ways, since none of us ever was tricked into thinking he cared about us. Just stop, all right? I know it's not that easy, but… none of this is your fault. Tell yourself that until you start to believe it."

Taniel sniffled and nodded.

"Promise?" Corsair asked with a faint smile.

"Promise. For real, this time. I'm really tired of lying. So finish telling me what happened."

Instead, Corsair kissed him, soft and sweet, before finally drawing back. "Eat, brat."

"All right, all right." Taniel sat back down, picked up the fork by the plate, and slowly ate.

"After I got back, and the general chaos that resulted from that was sorted, we realized nobody knew where you were. Kohar immediately set to tearing the place apart, but it was the dogs who found you in the end."

"The dogs?"

Corsair laughed. "You never took off the amulet I gave you. It worked exactly as intended. When we reached you, we found you and Vosgi on fire. Something I *never* want to see again. He was long dead, but you were hanging on and not nearly as severely burned as him. None of us knows why or how. We assume it must be something to do with the spells he laid on you, but we managed to pull you out and put out the fire. There were supplies aplenty stowed in that cave nearby, which allowed Kohar to stabilize you long enough to get off the mountain.

"Since then, you've been healing here. Been about a week. You've been in and out of consciousness, but your fever broke yesterday, so Kohar said you'd likely wake up soon. He was finally dragged off to sleep. He's supposed to relieve me in a few more hours. I'm supposed to get him the moment you wake." He smiled softly. "Wouldn't mind a few stolen minutes first, though, mean as it makes me."

"Kohar probably needs the rest badly, anyway. When our family… When everyone started falling sick, Kohar was the one who stayed by their bedsides, doing everything he could. I tried to keep things running, and when I couldn't, got work wherever I could. Gave me some distance and distraction that he didn't have."

"I'm surprised you two parted ways when it was all over."

"I think we needed to breathe, and we had different ways of doing that. We knew we'd find our way back to each other someday." Taniel blinked away fresh tears. "I just wish it hadn't been because of still more death."

"Come on, if you're not going to eat, you should get more rest," Corsair said, and pulled him from his seat and over to the bed. "Thinking like that won't help anything. Focus on how much worse off we'd be if you hadn't stood up to him, if you hadn't done the right thing, if you hadn't come here as quickly as you could to help. Stop punishing yourself. You've suffered enough, and you did more than most would to fix everything. I certainly would draw the line at setting myself on fire, you *dumbass*."

"It made sense at the time, I swear," Taniel muttered, and clung to Corsair as he was settled into bed. "I don't suppose you'd stay for a bit?"

"Of course." Corsair sat on the edge of the bed, removed his boots, then stood and stripped down to his leggings before climbing into bed. "Just let me know if I hurt you."

Taniel nodded and cuddled close as Corsair

pulled him in. He didn't care about pain right then; all of it was minor anyway. Even if it was severe, it would be well worth it to sleep right there curled up against Corsair, finally feeling sane and not so miserably alone.

*~*~*

"—both of you!"

"Sorry, Kohar, I meant to come get you once he fell asleep, I swear—"

Taniel sat up with a groan, pressing one hand to his aching head. "Kohar, shut up, you're giving me a headache already." He peeled his eyes open, lowered his hand—and whatever he was going to say was forgotten. "Kohar?"

"You're such a stupid fucking bastard," Kohar said as he pulled Taniel into a hug so tight it threatened his breathing.

"Can't breathe."

Kohar eased up slightly. "Do you know how it felt to see you like that! You're the only family I have left! Mom and Dad would *kill* me if I let you get your stupid self dead, you complete and utter dumbass."

"I love you too, and I'm sorry, I really really am," Taniel said, and hugged him tightly. "I just didn't want anyone else getting hurt."

Sitting back, Kohar wiped his face, scowling throughout. "Whatever. I'm going to be mad at you for the next six months, and if you so much as leave the castle without telling me—"

"All right, all right, all *right,* Mom. Gods above, I hope you never have children."

Kohar wrinkled his nose. "Forget that. Stop distracting me. How are you feeling?"

"Fine, especially considering I should be, um, well-cooked."

"Watch it," Kohar said, eyes narrowing.

"Look, I'm going to keep making jokes; you're going to have to get used to it."

"You're going to have to get used to my fist in your face."

"You couldn't throw a punch to save your life," Taniel retorted, "and your soldier boy isn't going to do it for you."

"No punching!" Corsair said. "Honestly, you two."

Kohar gave him a look. "You are not the slightest bit better with your siblings."

Corsair's face darkened. "That's not true; I actually punched them. My asshole cousin and everyone who defended him."

"I recall," Kohar replied dryly. "I was the one who patched you up when the tussle was over."

"Oh, my gods," Taniel said with a groan, burying his face in his hands. "Your family is never going to like me now." He was pretty sure there'd never been any chance of that, but it was definitely set in stone now.

"They will if they have any sense in their heads," Corsair replied.

"Precisely," Kohar added icily.

Taniel rolled his eyes. "Knock it off, both of you. Can we eat? I'm starving. I also want to get out of this room."

Kohar moved so he could climb out of bed. "Only if you tell me everything that happened from the time you broke your promise to the moment I found you almost burned to death."

"Never living that down," Taniel muttered as he quickly pulled on clean clothes. He'd really need a proper bath later, but for the moment, all he wanted was food.

Kohar frowned at him in that 'fretful mother' way of his, so much like their actual mother had once given them. Hilarious that Kohar was the one who didn't want children when he'd be so good at parenting.

That was all right. Taniel had every intention someday of forcing him into being an uncle.

"Are you certain—"

"Yes, Kohar. Stop fretting. Come on, I want real food and to see something beyond these four walls."

"You've barely been awake long enough to see these walls."

"Shut up."

Kohar heaved a sigh but followed along beside him, Corsair on the opposite side, leaving Taniel feeling very much like he was being escorted—watched. Not that he could blame them.

Downstairs, his stomach growled loudly as the smell of food struck him. Dragon stew night, perfect. He was going to eat six bowls, and every last slice of bread he could find, and to finish—

He slammed into Corsair's back, though when Corsair had stepped in front of him, Taniel had no idea.

"What do you think *you're* doing here?" Corsair asked in the coldest tones Taniel had ever heard from him. "Did you need another ass kicking?"

A garbled voice said, "No, one was more than enough, jackass. I came to talk—to apologize. We all did."

Taniel finally stepped around Corsair and stared at the group several paces away. Corsair's mom, the three who'd beaten him up, and a couple of others. They all looked shamefaced as they spied him.

"I don't hear any apologizing," Corsair snapped.

His mother huffed and pushed through the others to stand in front. "Master Taniel, what my sons and nephews did, what I allowed them to do, was unacceptable. We were afraid for Corsair, but that didn't give us leave to blame and hurt you. We apologize for acting the way we did and beg your forgiveness."

One by one, the others shuffled forward to give variations of her words. Around them, the hall had gone silent. Even Bedros and Warren watched intently.

"I can't say I enjoyed being beaten, and it still makes me a little wary to get too close to any of you, but I understand why you acted as you did. Corsair is safe, and Vosgi is dead exactly as I said he would be, so we'll just call it over and done with. I don't want to be the wedge between you and Corsair."

"You're too nice," Corsair said.

"Enough," Taniel said, poking him in the side. "Stop being stubborn and let's go eat."

Corsair scowled at his family a bit longer, then dropped his folded arms and turned away. "Fine. Everyone come eat. But one word—"

"Enough!" Taniel said, exasperated and amused all at once. He grabbed hold of Corsair's arm and dragged him away to their usual table, where a couple of the kitchen workers brought platters and bowls and plates to them, along with pitchers of beer that smelled faintly of strawberries. He hadn't thought that one would be ready for a couple more weeks.

He pulled a bowl of stew close and dug in, eating it faster than he could remember eating anything in a long time. Around him people laughed, but Taniel ignored it, entirely focused on the food.

When he'd finally eaten enough to slow down and actually enjoy it, he looked at the rest of the table, gaze landing on Corsair's brother or cousin or whatever he was. "Why hasn't anyone fixed your face?"

"Madame Karen refused to," the man grumbled.

"I see," Taniel said. "That seems unnecessarily vindictive."

Beside him, Corsair scowled. "No, it doesn't. Maybe this will get through your log-head that you need to watch that temper of yours."

"I get it, Corsair, all right?" the man said. "Back off, good grief."

"Enough, boys," the mom said. "I'm Petra by the way, and this is Tarmin." She pointed to the others. "Alex, Ray, and Verren."

"Tarmin and Alex are my useless brothers, and Ray and Verren are my useless cousins."

"Shut up, flounced-off-to-the-city boy," Ray said with a grin.

"Nice to meet you," Taniel said. "I really am sorry for all the trouble Vosgi caused."

"Rumor has it you set him on fire," Tarmin said.

Taniel shrugged. "Yes. Not an experience I want to repeat. Now let's have it: stories about little Corsair. I want them, and you were mean to me, so you can't refuse."

Corsair groaned as his relatives grinned evilly and started talking.

Castle Rehm Trilogy Fin

# ABOUT THE AUTHOR

Megan is a long time resident of queer romance, and keeps herself busy reading and writing it. She is often accused of fluff and nonsense. When she's not involved in writing, she likes to cook, harass her wife and cats, or watch movies. She loves to hear from readers, and can be found all over the internet.

meganderr.com
patreon.com/meganderr
pillowfort.io/maderr
meganderr.blogspot.com
facebook.com/meganaprilderr
meganaderr@gmail.com
@meganaderr

www.ingramcontent.com/pod-product-compliance
Ingram Content Group UK Ltd.
Pitfield, Milton Keynes, MK11 3LW, UK
UKHW041954190726
13854UKWH00005B/1964

9 798450 064604